D0638584

Praise for
Letters from War

"Mark Schultz has touched millions with his song 'Letters from War.' Now Mark's novel will take you deeper into the story, grabbing your imagination and taking you on an unforgettable journey of the heart."

—Karen Kingsbury, *New York Times* bestselling author of *Unlocked* and *Leaving*

"The first time I heard Mark Schultz's song 'Letters from War,' I was speechless. Now, seeing the heart of that message poured into a full-length novel, I'm not just speechless, but amazed at the sacrifice our men and women in uniform—and their families—so willingly make to protect our freedom. Thanks, Mark, for reminding us all of the cost of liberty."

—Dave Ramsey, host of *The Dave Ramsey Show*, bestselling author of *The Total Money Makeover*

"A compelling story of the love a mom, dad, and bride have for their soldier. *Letters from War* graphically reminds us of the price our soldiers and their families pay to protect our nation. You'll not be able to put this book down."

—Dr. Dennis Rainey, president of FamilyLife

"The first time I met Mark Schultz I heard him sing in Estes Park. He closed out his set with 'Letters from War,' accompanied by a very moving music video. I wept when I listened and watched the story unfold. What makes Mark special is that he is an advocate through song and story for the forgotten people of this world. He causes us to see our story in theirs, uniting through brokenness and hope. *Letters from War* is a must-read."

—Sandi Patty, Women of Faith speaker, most awarded female vocalist in Christian music history

"As Americans we understand and admire the courage and strength of our military, but now Mark Schultz has taken us into the hearts of these freedom fighters. We, as the reader, can almost feel the love, worry, and pain that they and their families experience during their service."

—Lee Greenwood, multi-platinum-selling recording artist, Grammy Award winner, composer/singer of "God Bless the USA"

"As a friend and a fan of Mark Schultz, I have always been amazed at his ability to tell a great story through his songs. With his new book, *Letters from War,* Mark shows that his storytelling extends far beyond his music. Once again, Mark tells a compelling story that is going to touch the hearts of those who read it."

—Matthew West, Grammy-nominated singer and songwriter

"Mark Schultz is the ultimate storyteller. Through his music and now his book, *Letters from War* touches our hearts, lifts our spirits, and honors our country."

—Tommy Spaulding, *New York Times* bestselling author of *It's Not Just Who You Know*

Letters from War

A NOVEL

Mark Schultz

with Travis Thrasher

HOWARD BOOKS
A DIVISION OF SIMON & SCHUSTER, INC.

New York   Nashville   London   Toronto   Sydney   New Delhi

Howard Books
A Division of Simon & Schuster, Inc.
1230 Avenue of the Americas
New York, NY 10020

Copyright © 2011 by Mark Schultz

All rights reserved, including the right to reproduce this book or portions thereof in any form whatsoever. For information address Howard Books Subsidiary Rights Department, 1230 Avenue of the Americas, New York, NY 10020.

First Howard Books paperback edition September 2011

HOWARD and colophon are trademarks of Simon & Schuster, Inc.

For information about special discounts for bulk purchases, please contact Simon & Schuster Special Sales at 1-866-506-1949 or business@ simonandschuster.com.

The Simon & Schuster Speakers Bureau can bring authors to your live event. For more information or to book an event, contact the Simon & Schuster Speakers Bureau at 1-866-248-3049 or visit our website at www.simonspeakers.com.

Designed by Jaime Putorti

Manufactured in the United States of America

10 9 8 7 6 5 4 3 2 1

Library of Congress Cataloging-in-Publication Data

Schultz, Mark, 1970–
 Letters from war : a novel / Mark Schultz ; with Travis Thrasher.
p. cm.
I. Thrasher, Travis, 1971–. II. Title.
PS3619.C4783L48 2011
813'.6—dc22
2010054015

ISBN 978-1-4391-9731-8
ISBN 978-1-4391-9732-5 (ebook)

Scripture quotations marked NLT are taken from the Holy Bible, New Living Translation, copyright © 1996. Used by permission of Tyndale House Publishers, Inc., Wheaton, Illinois 60189. All rights reserved. Scripture quotations marked NIV are taken from the Holy Bible, New International Version®, NIV®. Copyright © 1973, 1978, 1984 by Biblica, Inc.™ Used by permission of Zondervan. All rights reserved worldwide.

This book is dedicated to the men and women who have served in the military—past, present, here, or overseas—and to their families. We are humbled and grateful for the sacrifices you have made.

Prologue

THE LAST LETTER

The soldier wrestles to write words he knows will be his last.

He searches his heart, trying to find what he wants to say. After so many letters, this one needs to count.

This one needs to last.

There is no one definitive sentence or theme he needs to write. Yet he wants his family to know that he will always be there, that he will always love them.

Just because he is gone doesn't mean he has left them.

There is so much he wants to say. Things to share. About the places he's seen, the journey he's been on, the road he's headed toward. The pride in his heart for serving his country.

He knows the world is full of bad places filled with

bad men. He remembers his father telling him that. He remembers that was one of the reasons he decided to join the army.

Yet even in a world like this, there is hope. Hope is not confined to Tennessee or the United States of America. Hope can be found in the darkest of spots, in the prisons of people's souls.

He thinks of her face and smiles.

He loves her and wants the best for her. He can only imagine how many times she's prayed for his safety, a safety that won't hold.

Maybe God one day will tell her the reasons why.

Maybe God will fill her with renewed hope once he's gone.

He starts writing.

In a world full of endless rhetoric, he tries to convey a simple and eloquent truth.

I'm not writing to say good-bye. I'm writing to make a promise.

So he does.

Part One

LETTERS FROM HOME

Beth

The house creaks with memories.

Beth Thompson walks across the hall toward the room with the slightly open doorway revealing a sliver of light. She passes these empty rooms every time she comes up the stairs: Emily's room on the corner, James's next to it, the hibernating guest bedroom. Pictures of the children decorate the walls but there is no substitute for hearing their laughter and seeing their smiles.

It's good to have someone home.

She knocks gently, then nudges the door. She sees pink pajamas and remembers the toddler days as if they happened that morning.

"Hey," Emily says, her thumbs working on the cell phone, her gaze fixed on it.

"Busy?"

Her twenty-one-year-old daughter shakes her head. "Just saying hi to some friends."

"Any of them boys?"

Emily laughs. "No. Just men your age. Asking for my hand in marriage."

"Be nice to your mother. You haven't been home long enough to start abusing me."

"It's just Trish. She says hi."

"Tell her to come on over soon," Beth says.

"Oh, she will. She didn't have to get a job. Her parents love her."

"I can think of quite a few things for her to do around here."

"You invent things to keep busy."

Beth smiles. "It works."

Emily looks up at her mother. Taking the comment as a cue, she puts the phone on the bed and moves over so her mother can sit next to her.

"I thought you went to bed," Emily says, brushing a runaway strand of dark hair from her face.

"Not yet. Just reading."

"It always happens. I keep tellin' ya."

"What?"

"You slow down in the evening and get all gloomy and such. I think I need to buy you a dog."

"Only if a babysitter comes with it."

Emily stretches, then yawns. "What a day. I forgot how crazy our family is."

"I don't know which side is more dysfunctional—your father's side or mine."

"Can you believe Uncle Stuart?"

Beth shakes her head. "No."

"I think his jokes are as bad as his cooking."

"Sometimes I wonder how your father and Stu could be brothers."

"Me too."

"What if I had married him?"

"I would have run away at four," Emily says, grinning.

Beth takes in the room and notices how little it has changed over the years. Seeing her daughter's clothes littering the floor, makeup and jewelry and other belongings scattered on top of the dresser, the messiness all seeming to have its proper order, reminds Beth of high school days.

"What?"

"I haven't been in here in some time," she says.

"What about James's room?"

She shakes her head. Emily studies her the way a therapist studies a client.

"Is it tougher today than normal days?" Emily asks, the question and her tone surprising Beth.

She's already acting more grown-up and she hasn't even started her junior year yet. I'm not ready to have both of my children all grown-up.

"It would be if I had to celebrate Memorial Day by myself." She grips Emily's strong hand. "I'm glad you didn't go on that trip."

"Mexico is *so* overrated."

"Not when you're twenty-one."

"Have you ever been?"

"Yes, I was twenty-one at one point in my life."

Emily rolls her eyes. "I mean to Mexico."

"Me?" Beth laughs. "Please. I was married to your father by the time I was twenty. I'd barely been out of Tennessee by then."

"Don't give me this *aw shucks* business, Mom."

"I'm not. I'm just being honest."

"The parade was nice, wasn't it?"

"They always are. I just wish—the flowers were unnecessary."

"I had nothing to do with it."

"Emily . . ."

Her smile is so innocent, so beautiful, so much like her father's. "I swear. Everybody knows your story, Mom."

"It's our story."

"Yeah, I know. But I just . . ."

Beth waits for Emily to finish. She's used to the half thoughts and unfinished phrases, especially when Emily's talking about James.

"Maybe it's just—maybe I've come to a place where I finally have peace about it all."

They've had this conversation before. Beth knows how it can go. She is careful with her words. "That's good to hear."

"I just wish everybody didn't talk about the war like they're following it nonstop. Like they're all giving their take on it. That's all anybody talks about—the war, politics. Well, when Uncle Stu's not talking."

"I prefer listening to Stu over conversations about politics and war," Beth says.

"That whole al-Qaeda-versus-Taliban discussion—I wanted to curl up in the dishwasher. Most of them don't have a clue what they're talking about anyway."

For a while they don't say anything. Eventually Emily shifts deeper into her pillow and speaks with a soft voice. "Sometimes I dream about James. Like I'm talking to him. Then I wake up."

She's staring at the ceiling as if it's a star-filled sky on a cloudless night. Emily looks as if she's recalling a fond memory from just the other day, the kind of memory that makes one stop and smile.

"That's understandable."

Emily plays with her hair as she glances again at her mom. "What do you think that means?"

"That you miss him," Beth says, "just like the rest of us. Just like those watching the news on Afghanistan all day long as if they're going to get a glimpse of him on TV or something."

"Just like you writing those letters?"

The statement startles her. For a moment, Beth can't say anything.

"Sorry. I just—I saw you put one in the mailbox Saturday. You still write them on a regular basis?"

She nods.

Then Beth sees one of the saddest looks she's ever beheld on her daughter's face. It's not the childlike poutiness of Emily not getting her way, or the smart-aleck whimsy that usually accompanies her sarcasm. It's more of a strained heaviness that comes only with age and experience. Those beautiful blue eyes look lost at sea.

"It's okay," Beth says.

Emily doesn't say anything back. She tightens her lips in a forced smile.

Sometimes, there's really and truly nothing to say.

Sometimes, all one can do is sit holding hands with a loved one, lost in thought and memory.

———

The ritual is the same.

She turns off all the lights except those on the porch.

As if that one dim light right next to the rocking chair will be a guiding light in the darkness.

As if James needs it to find his way home.

She leaves it on for the simple fact that it's

something she *can* do. There are so many things she can't. She can't fly over there, strap on a gun and a backpack, and go searching for him the way Chuck Norris might. She's can't communicate with him in any manner or form. She can't even communicate with his officers. There has been limited interaction, and it's always been the same: cryptic information combined with government-speak.

What she can do is leave a light on, and she does that every night.

Heading back up the stairs, Beth notices the light in Emily's bedroom is off. She wonders if her daughter is asleep. Then she finds herself recalling the days she and her husband would tiptoe past her room, trying to be as quiet as possible. Some nights she would push James's door open to find him reading by flashlight or playing with his toys.

In her bedroom moments later, the taste of toothpaste still in her mouth, the face in the mirror looking older for some reason tonight, Beth kneels by her bed and prays. Maybe it's Emily being there or maybe it was the parade and the special presentation of flowers she received. Maybe it was the family gathering at the house that kept her busy and somewhat sane. Maybe it's none of those things. But for some reason, Beth prays a different prayer tonight.

She always prays for James and Emily.

Yet tonight, she also prays for herself, asking God for a little extra strength and wisdom.

Not that she hasn't asked for it before. But with Emily around, she's trying to act stronger yet doing a miserable job at it.

James might be gone. Either in another country or in heaven. She doesn't know.

What she does know is that her twenty-one-year-old daughter is alive and kicking. Emily is strong and alert and insanely perceptive, meaning Mom needs to be strong.

Whatever that means.

After praying, Beth finds the stationery and realizes she needs to get more soon. A familiar hand pens a familiar phrase on the cream-colored paper.

May 30, 2011

Dear James,

There's something about Memorial Day that I don't like. I don't want to acknowledge it, not when it comes to you. I don't want to admit that you're gone.

That's why today has been bittersweet. It's a day of remembering, yes. A day to reflect and to memorialize.

Yet for me, it feels like a day in which I'm supposed to stop hoping.

Your sister misses you. It's not in what Emily says but it's in what she doesn't say. I can see it in her eyes and in her expression. Something's missing. That mischievous part you always brought out in her. She's used to being the nagging little sister who always wanted to do what her older brother was doing. Her role of only child is a strange one for both of us.

I wish you could have been here today with the family as they gathered in the house. It was nice to have so many here. I think some came because they feel like it's time to embrace the idea that you're gone. Honestly, James—today had the feeling of a wake, strange as it might sound. Maybe it's because all of us know that in just a few months, it will be two years. Two whole years since you went missing.

How I dearly wished you could have walked in and shocked everyone, like the ghost of Christmas past or present or even future.

I wonder if you're with your father, watching me write words in vain, wondering when I'll stop. Do you know that sometimes I'll wake up in the middle of the night, worried I didn't finish my daily letter, worried that you're waiting for it? Maybe this keeps me going. Maybe this keeps me hopeful.

To be honest, I'm running on empty most of the time. Most of those at the house today wouldn't guess it. At least I don't think they would. But that's how I've been feeling. I'm sure Emily knows, but she's smart enough not to probe too much.

A gnawing fear surfaces again and again. I wonder if you're hurting. That's what bothers me the most—to think you're somewhere suffering. I can deal with the news of your passing because I know you'll be in a better place, not hurting. But the thought of you in pain . . .

A mother shouldn't imagine her child in pain.

Then I remember that the reason you are where you are—the reason for all of this—is to keep other mothers from feeling this burden, from sharing this ache.

You're not doing this to be a hero. I know that, James. You want to help others, and you're doing exactly that.

Still, the questions build.

Every day I wonder if the dam will burst.

Yet every day the good Lord gets me through.

Sometimes I don't know what I'd do without Emily. God

knows that she and I can be like oil and vinegar, yet God also knows what I can and can't handle.

Today is a day for remembering, and you shine bright in our minds.

I see your spirit strong like your father's and tender like mine.

I see your smile glowing in the summer sun right before you said good-bye.

I see so many things and think there is a reason I keep these memories and hopes and dreams alive, James.

In my heart, you are alive.

In my heart, I believe I will see you again.

I don't know if all prayers are equal, but I do believe that a mother's prayers carry weight. God hears them, and He grants peace in the most unlikely of places.

Maybe even in some hidden cave in Afghanistan.

I continue to pray for you. Know that.

I love you.

If possible, be safe. And be strong.

                                        Your mother

She folds the letter and slips it in the envelope, then addresses it and places it on the dresser for tomorrow's mail. As she does, she sees one of the framed photos watching her, grinning in the silence.

It's a picture of James with his father, Richard.

If love was four by six inches in brilliant color, this would be it.

The familiar ache comes like the gentle kiss of a child, unabashed.

Sometimes, the more you love, the more you hurt.

It shouldn't be that way, but in a fallen and broken world, there are many things that shouldn't be.

Beth accepts it, even embraces it. She would rather hurt knowing the love exists than never be able to picture it at all.

In the darkness moments later, under the covers in an ocean of a bed, she thinks of a land she's never seen before and wonders if he's there.

Doing what she's doing.

Waiting and wondering.

———

Every weekday morning, the sunrise competes with her grandson's smile.

Beth watches Richie pounding a plastic toy into another as he sits in his hunkered-down stance on the worn carpet. The wide eyes and healthy cheeks and giggling demeanor never hint at the truth behind this little man. The boy doesn't know the father he's missing, the father he's never seen in person. The father who doesn't even know his name.

Perhaps some grandmothers wouldn't be able to move on from this fact. But now that Richie can walk, Beth doesn't have time to sit around moping about missing soldiers. Instead, she relishes these moments and reflects on how much Richie's little round face resembles his father's.

A cackle comes out of the toddler's mouth as he gnaws on the plastic car. Richie is only a year and a half old. They never decided on a name, so after James went missing, the choice of names fell to Britt. She decided to name him Richard, after his grandfather. Everybody has since designated him Richie or little Rich.

"I know—that's pretty cool, huh?"

Richie's playing with a new toy that Beth brought over. She can't help herself. This is her first grandchild and she can't help spoiling him.

You can't spoil someone who's missing half his life. It's impossible.

Every weekday morning, Beth comes over to this house to watch Richie while his mommy goes to work. Britt usually comes back home around one in the afternoon. It's the least Beth can do. In fact, these visits are something she's grown used to, something she's started to need.

The phone rings and Beth answers it, already knowing who it is.

"Everything going okay?"

A year and a half and Britt is still more worried than she should be.

"He's in a great mood today."

"He's always in a great mood when Grandma brings him new toys," Britt says with a smile in her voice.

"It was on sale at the store. I couldn't say no."

"I just realized that there's nothing to eat for lunch."

"It's fine. We'll find something. We can always go out."

"I'm sorry."

"It's fine. Please."

Beth ends up telling Britt about something new that Richie did this morning. She can understand the extra anxiety in her daughter-in-law. Anybody who has something traumatic happen, like the death of a spouse (or in this case, the possibility of death), will surely be left with oversensitivity.

"I'll try working on that stain in the carpet sometime later," Beth says. "That was quite the explosion."

"I didn't mean to leave you with that mess."

"You never forget how to clean up messes like that. Richard could do anything on a battlefield, but give him a messy diaper and he suddenly became completely inept."

For a brief second, there's a pause. Beth quickly fills in the silence.

"Don't rush home. We're going to take a nice little stroll around the neighborhood after lunch."

After getting off the phone, Beth looks at the wedding picture of James and Britt. Who would ever have guessed that a little over a year after it was taken, this beautiful picture of love would be cracked in half?

She feels tugging at her leg. Glancing down, Beth sees Richie with his mouth wide open and smiling.

Who would have guessed that three months after that, God would bless us with this strong bundle of love?

He's still not too big to pick up. Almost, but not there yet.

Beth lifts Richie and then shows him the picture.

"That's your mommy and daddy. Do you know that?"

She wants to say that he's going to see his daddy soon, that his daddy loves him, that his daddy's going to come and make things better. But Beth can't say any of those things.

He's only one and a half, but I can't lie to him.

"You look just like he did, you know that?"

It could be a blessing or a curse, depending on how you looked at it.

Holding this precious child in her arms, Beth can only think of it as an amazing gift.

"Come on, let's go try to clean up that mess you made in your room. Okay?"

———

She stares at the picture of the perfect family standing in front of her in the atrium of the church.

They're perfect because they're together, all the members still intact.

The music has finally stopped streaming out of the open doors of the converted gym. Holding on to a church program, Beth can't help smiling as she watches the playful jostling between siblings. She waits for Josie as the mother of four makes sure the rest of her family knows the plan. It appears the only one of the group who needs special attention is the father.

"Maybe we'll just go to Denny's," Phil tells his children.

There is a collective groan as the man looks at the two of them and laughs.

"Be kind to the kids," Josie tells him.

"They really do have good food. If you weren't so health-conscious maybe you'd try it out."

"My idea of a good breakfast isn't a Grand Slam."

"Hey—don't knock it till you've tried it!"

Beth watches Phil talking to the teenagers the way a youth pastor might interact with his kids. There is an unmistakable bond visible between the father and his children. She takes in the scene and studies it, her eyes more focused than they were ten minutes earlier during the pastor's sermon.

The kids laugh at their father's jokes and joke back. A relaxed and joyous banter bounces among them, the kind that contradicts the typical image of a typical father with teenage children. The father glances up at Beth.

"How are you doing today?" he asks.

"I'm doing well," she says. "Thanks."

It might be easy to be envious or bitter, but she knows that these two things are exactly like the cancer that killed Richard. They grow in silent, dark spaces. If not caught, they are deadly.

"So what are you in the mood for?" Josie asks her after they say good-bye to the rest of the gang.

"Something healthy," Beth says. "Like a hamburger."

———

The women agree where to meet and separate in the parking lot. The Sunday after Memorial Day is hot, and even though the drive to the restaurant takes just ten minutes, the air conditioner in Beth's car is still blowing mostly warm air. The SUV is only a few years old, but she is starting to wonder if she needs to get it checked. With everything going on, she doesn't want to deal with taking the car in for a tune-up.

That's someone else's responsibility.

The errant thought surprises her. She imagines it's probably having Emily home, a nonstop voice that never ceases to surprise her.

She thinks of Emily and calls her on her cell.

"I notice you didn't come home last night."

"Yeah, I met a guy at the restaurant," Emily says. "He lives in a crummy trailer in the middle of the woods."

"Stop it."

"I told you I was going over to Trish's place after work."

She's glad to hear that Emily doesn't sound too tired.

"I missed you in church."

"We were up late last night."

"I hope you weren't being foolish."

Emily sighs. "Just because I didn't go to church doesn't mean I was up to no good."

"I thought Trish went to church."

"She does. They went this morning. I came back home. I'm sitting on the deck."

"You're home?"

"Yeah."

"Why didn't you tell me?" Beth asks. "I could've changed my lunch plans."

"It's no big deal."

"You didn't want to go to church with Trish?"

"Not really."

This new air of—what is it?—indifference, perhaps nonchalance, toward church is something new. It's been there ever since she came back from college.

But now's not the time.

"I won't be long," Beth says.

"Enjoy yourself. I just started a new book today."

"Anything I'd like?"

"It's by Dennis Shore."

"Ooh. Too scary for me. I don't need anything else to keep me awake at night. I have enough already."

"Why do you think I'm reading it in the daytime?"

———

Throughout lunch, she can tell that Josie is digging, probing, trying a little harder than usual.

And then:

"There's nothing wrong with letting go."

The statement slaps her across the face. In stunned silence, Beth hears the soft echoes of conversation in the dining room, the familiar clinking of silverware against china, the footsteps of a server rushing by. For a moment she's frozen in time, not sure where the comment came from, not sure what to say back.

"And I don't say that to hurt you in any way."

Beth tightens her lips and takes a sip of her iced tea. "Then maybe you shouldn't have said it. Because it hurts."

"It's been two years."

"It will be two years in August."

"A lot of folks are worried, Beth."

"So am I."

"They're worried about you."

For a moment, she glances down at her hand. Her ring is there and will always be. She notices how pale and bony her hands and arms have become, how old she's starting to look now that looks are the last thing on her mind.

"There are plenty of more important things for people to worry about."

"I'm just telling you the truth."

"Just because something is true doesn't mean it needs to be shared."

Josie shakes her head. Perhaps Beth should have seen this coming. Maybe it's a long time coming. But letting go means giving up, and she has no plans to give up.

"Please—don't be angry."

"I'm not angry. Hurt, yes, but not angry."

"I can't imagine what these past two years have been like."

"I'm not asking you to. I'm not asking anybody to imagine."

"But we're here alongside you. You know that. We're praying just like you're praying."

A server comes and asks if they want anything more to drink. Beth smiles and tells him they're fine.

"Didn't we have this same conversation once before?"

"Beth—"

"Didn't we? But the thing is, I needed that conversation. You were right to tell me it was time to move on. Because Richard wasn't ever coming back. It doesn't mean I took all your advice. I mean, it's not like I'm hitting the dating scene the way you encouraged me to do."

"I still don't think that's a bad idea."

"This is different. This is far different. I will never let go, Josie. Not until someone comes to my door and tells me where James is. I managed to move on when Richard died. And if it's God's will, I'll move on again when the time comes."

"Maybe that time is now."

"Is there something wrong with believing? Is hope such a bad thing in these dark and cynical days?"

Josie glances down at her plate, thinking for a moment. "It's one thing to have hope and trust in God. But it's another to let it go on too long."

"And what? Become an obsession?"

"What about Emily?"

Beth would have already left the conversation far behind if it had been anybody else. But Josie was family. She had been there and continued to be there and this was just one more way Josie was trying to help.

She has no idea what she's asking me to do.

"Emily is strong."

"That's because she has your genes and you're one of the strongest people I've ever met," Josie says, moving in toward her. "But sometimes you have to be strong enough to—"

"No."

"Beth, please."

"Please what? I know you're trying to be a friend. And friends are honest with one another. Phil and you have been a wonderful support—your whole family has. But this is something that I can't—I won't—do. It's not like some bad habit I need to give up."

"But it's okay if you—"

"He's my son. He is my son."

Josie sits back in her chair, her face drained, her shoulders slumped. Beth wonders if she was a little too emphatic with her last statement.

"Would anybody like some dessert?" the server comes and asks.

Beth moves her hand across the table and squeezes Josie's.

"Let's split one. Come on. It'll be good for us."

———

Waiting is worse than knowing.

Beth thinks this as she sits in the comfortable armchair attempting to read the worn Bible in her lap. Like a blanket on a cold night, the verses wrap around her, keeping her heart and soul warm.

Yet for a moment, she slides off her glasses and rests them on the page.

Maybe Josie is right. Maybe it's time to move on.

She tries to do what she should.

Be still in the presence of God, and wait patiently for Him to act.

The sound of a fan nearby is the only thing she can hear. *Nine out of ten people reading at this time of night might drift off with that engine purring in their ears,* Beth thinks. But worry carries a much louder sound, and it's a constant whine she hears all day long.

Oh, Lord, I am calling to You. Please hurry!

Two years is a long time to call. A long time to wait. A long time to ask for assistance.

Hear my cry, for I am very low.

She wouldn't be human if she didn't have moments like this. Beth knows this. She will always be a mother.

She could be the first human being to ever step foot on Mars, but she'd still say her crowning achievement were those two beautiful and blessed babies.

I am losing all hope.

David knew and he knew it well. His words weren't all glowing praises to God. Many of them were the desperate longings of a man broken and bruised and waiting.

Waiting.

Beth sighs and slips her glasses back on.

She continues reading the psalms.

She wonders if James is indeed alive, and if so if he can recall David's words.

Have mercy on me, O God, have mercy! I look to You for protection.

Does James call out morning, noon, and night for God's protection?

I will hide beneath the shadow of Your wings until this violent storm is past.

When will the storm pass? When will the clouds lift and the sun shine down on shadows and allow her to finally know? To finally see the truth?

My heart is confident in You, O God.

Can she say the same?

Beth isn't sure.

She wants to but she can't say that God looks through her heart and believes her.

Just as she's about ready to turn off the lights downstairs, the door opens and she hears Emily coming in.

At least she doesn't have to wait for her daughter to come home.

At least one prayer was answered on this night.

———

"Why do you have to worry so much about what I'm doing?"

"Why do *you* have to keep it some big secret?"

"Why do you think I have secrets?"

"If you don't have secrets, why can't you just tell me what you're up to?"

Conversations like this are like riding a carousel, Beth thinks. *Eventually you end up getting dizzy and nauseous if you don't step off.*

Emily seems a bit more irritable this Friday morning. She's got the college look down pat, with bags under youthful eyes, sweatpants and a college tee on, a bowl in her lap as she watches one of the morning shows.

With a mouth full of cereal, Emily says she's not keeping anything a secret.

"Then where were you?"

"Are you going to be like this all summer?"

"Are you?" Beth asks.

The morning talk show host seems far more important to Emily than her mother does.

"I was just asking."

Emily turns around on the sofa to look her way. "I went over to Trish's house, then we went to someone's house. We went to a bar—it was just silly. Country music, nothing but a bunch of rednecks. Went back to Trish's to watch a movie."

"What was so wrong with telling me that?"

"You've been overly worried ever since I got that job at O'Malley's. You wanted me to get a job, didn't you?"

"I would have preferred something a little less—"

"Wild? Sorry, the convent didn't ever call me back. I can become a nun next summer."

"I don't need to explain the types of people that end up at bars," Beth says.

"Did I do something wrong last night? Did I go AWOL or something?"

"Don't."

"Don't what?" Emily asks.

This time she's the one who doesn't reply. Beth goes back in the kitchen.

Her daughter knows how to shut down a conversation.

Loading the dishwasher, Beth worries about pushing Emily. She worries about going into enemy territory. She worries that if they go there, they won't be able to come back. They've been there before.

Words are like land mines. There's nothing you can do once you've triggered them.

When Emily comes in with her bowl, Beth offers to take it.

"I wasn't doing anything bad. Okay?"

"Okay," she tells Emily.

"Mom, nothing's going to happen to me."

"I know."

"I think you're more worried when I'm around than when I'm at school."

"When you're at school, I keep my mouth shut. I have to."

"I'm glad you're not like some of the mothers. They're texting and sending their kids messages on Facebook."

"Why not just call?" Beth asks with a smile.

"Why not just smother?" Emily says.

"What am I going to do with you?" Beth gives Emily a hug. "You won't ever understand until you have your own child."

"Yeah, but I don't think you necessarily want that to happen now, huh?" Emily laughs in the same mischievous way she has since she was two.

—

She remembers the first time silence covered her.

It was when James had been in Iraq for only two months. She had already spoken to him on the phone several times as well as received letters. Yet on the day he had told her he would be calling, there was nothing. All attempts to contact him didn't work either. She got Emily involved, asked her to try to e-mail, yet no response came.

A day was one thing.

But as each day passed, she felt as if a rope was attached to her legs and was pulling her into a deep black ocean. Her hands were holding on to the rails of the boat, but each day the weight grew heavier, her grip more unsure, the burning in her hands and legs more severe.

Waiting is wearisome.

Waiting is life on pause, watching on the sidelines, restless and troubled.

Bible verses comforted her and prayers helped and Emily tried to encourage and family and friends supported, but . . .

None of those things diminished the overwhelming, oppressive nature of waiting.

She compared it to watching a sky slowly begin to turn black, bit by bit, until night was there while everybody was telling her it was only noon.

Finally, the phone call came and it was James.

His unit had been put in a temporary blackout due to a soldier's being killed in combat. The army did this to make sure that the family would be notified properly instead of discovering the death online or hearing about it via e-mail from a long-lost acquaintance.

For the first few minutes that James was on the other line telling her what happened, Beth was on her knees.

On her knees because of both the fear of the phone call and the fear of God.

She was thankful for both of those things, and the tears showed her gratitude.

"You okay, Ma?" James asked her.

And she told him she was, trying to hide the terror that had encased her for those few days.

Little did Beth know that those few days were just an appetizer for this feast of grief.

She'd gotten just a taste—a nibble—but not even that prepared her for these past two years.

Now she knew how quickly she could go underwater, how dark the liquid could be, how cold and silent it felt under the surface.

As soon as she heard that James was missing in action, she decided to be especially present in her own life. Beth had remained busy and on guard and prayerful and mindful.

The Bible and prayers fueled her. Family and friends kept her sane. She needed to keep moving and keep trekking. Keep "humping," as Richard used to say.

But two years of moving and wandering was a long

time. Beth knew that her energy and her sanity were almost depleted.

She kept waiting for relief to come. And relief could come only in the form of an answer. Any answer.

Lord, keep me strong. Keep me going. Keep me in Your arms as long as possible.

Those were the only kinds of words that kept her going.

———

"I tried, Beth. God knows I'm trying. But it's not like riding a bike. It takes a little more work than that."

"You're not being graded. That's the beautiful thing about it. Everybody comes with his own faults and failures. That's the blessed thing about grace."

Beth changes the phone from one ear to the other. She's been on the phone with Marion DiGiulio for half an hour. The Friday-afternoon phone call came without fail. For the last six months, it's been a constant, just like the letters. Normally Marion calls saying she has unlimited minutes to use on her cell phone.

Even though they've only met once, Beth considers the woman on the other end of the phone one of her closest friends.

So few understand what we're going through.

"My father was good about teaching us about sin. The grace thing I don't know much about."

Beth knows that these phone conversations have evolved. From the start, it was simply about keeping in touch with the mother of the soldier who went missing with James. Sergeant Francisco DiGiulio from Chicago, whom most everybody called Frankie, was with James's convoy when the ambush happened. At first the two women would simply compare notes. Now they compare lives.

"My father lived by example," Beth replies. "He was a good man who went to the same church most of his life. He went to be with the Lord a few years ago. I could not believe how many people came up to me to tell me how he touched their lives. I couldn't believe it because my father was a quiet man, understated in so many ways. I guess that's where I got my assurance from. I saw it lived out in my parents' lives."

"Faith is harder to find after losing it."

"I can believe that."

These Friday conversations that used to be about what the army knew, what they had been told, and how they were both coping had recently morphed into the subject of faith. Many times Marion commented in her more emotional moments on how well Beth seemed to be managing everything. Beth didn't always agree, citing the fact that she struggled daily just like any mother would. But that led to the discussion of how Beth was relying on God through this.

I'm a lot like Dad. He was never one to talk about it unless someone brought it up.

"I had an awful thought the other night," Marion said. "I thought that maybe this thing with Frankie and James was something God brought to bring me to Him. And right after I thought that, I got up and said, 'Uh-uh, no way.' I told God that if *that's* the way He was trying to get my attention, I didn't want any part of it."

"That's the scariest part for me."

"What?" Marion asks.

"Not knowing why. Not understanding why certain things happen."

"It's because this world is ugly and there are people who only want to destroy."

"Not everything is ugly," Beth says. "I saw that picture you sent us, the card with your family picture on it. That's beautiful."

"I have pretty children, don't I?"

"You do."

"Frankie should've been in that shot. We took it at his little sister's wedding. He should've been there."

"I have to believe there was a reason this happened," Beth says. "Or, at the very least, that God is in control."

"I'm used to being in control."

She laughs. "I think all mothers are. But this world shows us that ultimately we're not in control."

"Having children grow up tells me that," Marion

says with a bit more of a midwestern accent in her voice. "They grow up and do stupid things."

"Some grow up to be heroes."

There is a long pause.

"Sometimes I don't know which is worse," Marion says.

"What?"

"Having a son that's a delinquent, or having a son who's a hero."

—

"I just want to know the truth."

The craziest image comes to mind as she closes her eyes. She thinks of Jack Nicholson in military dress barking "You can't handle the truth!" at her. *A Few Good Men* was on TBS the other night, and she watched it for the tenth time. Something about watching people in that world gives her comfort, even if the world depicted was more Hollywood than military.

The voice on the other end of the phone is no Jack Nicholson, nor does he bark.

"Mrs. Thompson, there's nothing more I can tell you."

She's heard this, she *knows* this, yet she still waits for a response.

This is something she does on a regular basis, talking to different people in different departments hoping to find the Holy Grail of information. Hoping someone will whisper on the line that they know something they shouldn't tell her, that the army knows where James is and is about to rescue him.

That's Hollywood I'm hoping to talk to, she realizes.

This is just a small something she can do on a biweekly basis. It remains a part of her to-do list, just like cleaning the house and taking out the garbage and paying bills and getting her lawn maintained.

And yes, checking to see if the army has any more information on my one and only son who's been lost for two years.

Two years can pass by in a blink when you're a newlywed or a new parent or a new employee. But when it comes to grief, two years can seem like an eternity. Two years can feel like a Groundhog Day of gloom. The seasons might pass outside, but the season inside of you never changes; it only grows colder and darker with each passing sunset.

Beth thanks the man on the other end who is just doing his job and is doing it with compassion. The world is full of so many uncompassionate clubs, she knows, but the army is not one of them. They know how to take care of their own, even when the answers their own are looking for aren't there.

For a minute Beth thinks about her recent conversation with Marion, then thinks back to her women's group at church the other day, full of mothers complaining about their children. One complained that her sons never came around anymore. Another mother said she didn't get along with her son-in-law and therefore never saw her daughter. Beth shared a little about her own relationship with her daughter, but in the back of her mind she couldn't believe the insensitivity of these women. Maybe they assumed she had moved on. Maybe they had forgotten about it.

Everybody is selfish when it comes time to talk about their prayer needs. Everybody wages their own daily war.

The most comforting words and support had come from others who had been there, even a few who were in the same boat she was. She got an e-mail out of the blue forwarded by an army captain. It came from the father of a marine who had been missing in action for over three years until they discovered him dead. He had never given up hope, and the father told her to do the same.

> Just because they discovered Riley dead doesn't mean I regret hoping and believing that he was alive those three years. Those years made me a better man and drew me closer to the Lord. I don't have all the answers, but I do know that God has given me peace.

The words from Riley's father continue to haunt her. They also conflict with Josie's urging her to let go.

Beth stares at the window looking out to her backyard, but she's in a place far away from there. A place she doesn't even know or recognize but simply feels.

She shakes her head and then turns and strides upstairs, knowing that the moment she slows down is the one where she'll be crippled and unable to keep moving.

Step by step.

Day by day.

———

"Mom?"

"Yes?"

Emily walks into the bedroom as Beth finishes washing her face. Her daughter sits on the edge of the bed.

"I thought you were asleep," Emily says.

"I was. For a while. There's nothing on television. How was work?"

"Slow. They let me go home early. Made a whopping thirty bucks in tips."

"It's a weeknight."

"Tell me about it. So I wanted to tell you what happened."

Beth folds up some clothes and places them in an armchair in the corner of her bedroom, then sits next to Emily.

"What's wrong?"

"Nothing. It's not about work. It's just—well, I don't know if it's wrong. Maybe it is. That's what I want you to tell me."

Beth has learned to control her thoughts. By now Richard would have been asking for the name and address of the boy. Then grabbing his gun.

"What do you need to know?" Beth asks.

"I lost Daddy's letter."

There is no question which letter this is. She simply asks, "When?"

"I don't know exactly. I thought it was here at home, but I've searched my entire room twice and I can't find it. Part of me thinks—wonders—maybe I took it off to school. I think it might have been in a bag. But that's gone. I don't know."

"It's okay."

"If I lost it?"

"Things happen."

"Yeah, but—what if Dad's looking down on me and sees how dumb I was to lose something like that?"

Beth puts her arm around Emily. "I'm sure he wouldn't think you were dumb to lose it. Maybe he'll manage to put it across your path."

"I can't believe I lost it."

"Do you remember what it says?"

Emily rolls her eyes.

"I'm just asking," Beth says.

"Of course I do."

"Then that's all that counts."

"Yeah, but one day, when I'm old and senile, I might start to forget."

"Then write down the words you remember."

"Is that why you write to James?"

She thinks for a minute, rubbing her dry hands together. "He was the one who started writing to me. I asked him to and he obliged. But he always said that he wanted to be like his father in that regard. He even wrote to you a few times too, right?"

"Yeah."

"Maybe it's a way to carry on a tradition."

"I bet he did a better job keeping track of his letters than I do."

"That's because he wasn't as busy as someone like you."

"Are you putting me on?"

She smiles at her daughter. "Just a little."

"I actually started to cry today thinking I'd lost that letter. Thinking how disappointed Dad might be. Thinking how stupid I was."

"The important thing is that you remember what it says, that you keep the message it contains."

"You didn't read it?"

"Your letter?" Beth asks. "No. That was between your father and you."

"He said in the letter that when I turned twenty-one, you're supposed to start giving me a weekly allowance of two hundred dollars."

"Oh really?"

"Yeah, totally," Emily says with an amused look on her face.

"That's funny, because in my letter he said not to believe a word you say until you're twenty-five."

"Twenty-five?"

"Yes. So you have four more years."

"I wonder what he said to James," Emily says.

"Probably that he was going to pray for him, now that he was outnumbered by the females in the house."

James

AUGUST 17, 2000

The cap was a faded and ugly shade of orange, but James believed it was the most beautiful thing he'd ever seen. He'd found it an hour earlier in the garage on the neatly organized shelf. It belonged to his father. James could confidently say the Vols cap belonged to him now.

It felt heavy in his hands as he studied it. Even though his father had worn it to dozens of games over the years, James had a hard time picturing him in it. He didn't know why. Even with the big framed photo of his father back at the church, James kept forgetting what his father looked like. *Sometimes,* he thought, *you neglect to really look at someone when you see them every day.*

The room was quiet. Mom and Emily were somewhere downstairs, which was good. He didn't want to be bothered. He didn't want to be asked how he was feeling. He wasn't exactly sure how he was feeling, and even if he was, he wouldn't have told the person asking. The only person he'd have told was the one person he couldn't.

The last Tennessee game they'd gone to was the last home game of the year, Vols versus Vanderbilt. Even though they didn't end up winning a championship as they had the year before, the Vols still had a good team and beat Vandy by twenty-eight. James and his father had kept their father-son outings intact, even though his dad had started showing definite signs that he was sick.

Grandpa gave Dad this cap.

James could picture his grandfather's face at the funeral. A blank sheet of white. Nothing there, like some ghost passing in broad daylight. The image shook James even more than seeing his father in the casket. Grandpa knew what James did. That body—the one that failed him so early in life—*that* wasn't Dad.

He's somewhere else and he happened to forget to give me this cap so he reminded me when I was in the garage. He reminded me by causing the light to shine right on what first looked like a big tangerine with a white T on it.

James was going to try on the cap but then heard knocking. He felt caught, as if he were holding a can of beer or a cigarette in his hand. He managed to fling the hat across the room to his desk and miss it by an inch when the door opened.

"James? You in there?"

"Yeah."

"Can I come in?"

"Yeah."

His mother looked strange in black since she never wore it. Her blond hair stood out against the shoulders of the dress.

"How are you doing?"

"I'm okay," he said.

"What were you looking for in the garage?"

"Just looking around."

His mother glanced around the room, then noticed the cap. She picked it up and placed it on his desk, then sat down on the bed next to him.

"If it were up to your father, he would've been buried in that cap and his jersey."

James forced a smile and glanced at the carpet. His mother moved to face him.

"Do you know that when I told Richard for the first time I was pregnant, for the longest time he didn't want to hope for a son? I'd bring it up and he kept saying that we were going to have a girl, he was sure of it. We didn't find out, you know. So when you were born, your father just had this look—this look that I'd never really seen before. I'd seen glimpses. At Vols games, for instance.

Or when he was in his uniform. But nothing compared to that moment he held you in his arms and finally could see with his own eyes that he was holding his little boy."

A knot the size of a grapefruit quivered in James's throat. He looked away from his mom. He didn't want her to see the emotion in his face, the sadness and regret and hurt. James needed to be strong like his father. James needed to be strong for his family.

"James." Her voice cracked and he looked at her. "I just spoke with your sister. I told her the same thing I'm going to tell you. My parents are still alive, so I don't know exactly how you feel. All I know is this: there's a reason that God took your father. We might never know that reason. But I know and I believe there is one. I want you to know that I'm here and that I love you. You understand?"

He nodded and tried desperately to hold back the tears. He felt as if he was on the edge of a slippery, muddy canyon holding on even while inch by inch he slipped closer to dropping off. His hands were sweaty as he clenched them to avoid shaking.

"I have something for you. Something your father wanted me to give you."

She gave him a long, white sealed envelope. It trembled when he took it.

"I didn't read it. He wrote one for each of us."

James nodded again, looking at the wall, unsure

what to say. He wasn't about to start reading it in front of his mom.

"I'm sorry, James. I'm sorry that he's gone."

There wasn't anything else to do but hug her. He wasn't touchy-feely. Hugs always made him feel childish and silly. Yet this was all he could think to do.

The hug lasted a long time. More than anything, it felt important.

"Why don't you come down in a little while? We'll be in the kitchen. Grandma and Grandpa are coming over soon."

James watched her go out and close the door behind her. He hesitated to open the letter, unsure about reading words from a man now dead, afraid of how they might deepen the wound he felt.

Then slowly, carefully, he opened the envelope and pulled out the paper inside.

He recognized the orderly handwriting as he opened the folded letter.

My dearest James:

The last thing in the world you need now is more words. I am sure you will have heard enough by the time you read this letter.

But, Son, I don't write for your today. I write for your tomorrow. I write for the times when I should be there but can't be. I write for the times when the world won't make sense and I should be the one to make some sense of it.

Life doesn't make sense, James. Not this tiny little patch of life that we're given. But life is a gift, and when God decides that it's our time, there's nothing we can do. We need to be thankful for what we've been given so far.

Let me ask something of you.

Do not be sad. Be strong.

Do not let despair weigh you down. When you read these words, it might sound easy. Yet it may be tempting to wallow in what could have been. Instead, wake up tomorrow and be thankful. Know you are alive for a reason; you have a responsibility.

I know you are twelve, but I tell you these things as if you were a man. I wish I had time to watch you grow into one.

Your responsibility is to take care of your mother and your sister. Do not ask how. You will learn how. I know you can do this because I know you. I know your heart.

You are strong, James. You are like your mother that way. I might be the one who served in the military but your mother is the one who showed her true strength.

God will watch over the family and I hope that I will be able to as well. Your mother and sister will need your help.

Do I ask too much on this day? No. Because you don't have to start today.

Today you start with yourself. Those feelings I know are inside of you. Pray, James. I know you have heard us say this time and time again, but pray.

I remember what it was like to hear orders from our commander in chief. Sometimes I wondered what it would be like to stroll into his tent and ask to sit down and talk with the man.

Praying is like that, times infinity.

You are able to stand before your Maker and have His attention. You can do this any time you want. He does not always answer and when He does, it might be in His own way. But He hears you. He sees and loves you, James. So speak to Him.

When the time comes, you will take care of the family. I know that.

I already said the things I needed to say to you, but, Son, know how proud I am to have lived long enough to have spent time with you. Know how fortunate I am to have loved you long enough to be able to let you go.

Know how blessed I am to have gotten to know my son.

Follow God, Son, for He will never let you down. You will let yourself down, but do not let that stop you.

Follow your passion and your heart. Take that hurt and confusion and build it into something meaningful.

I pray that God blesses you with a long and healthy life. But remember that this life is just a tour of duty. It's a minute tour compared to the long journey ahead.

I have already started mine, and I believe with everything in me that if I could share what I see and feel now, you would be happy for me.

I wish I could tell you what I'm seeing and feeling, but I can't.

I can tell you this.

Do not fear. Fear is of the enemy. There is nothing good about it. Do not be foolish, but neither live with fear. There is only one Person who controls everything, and He states, "Fear not, for I am with thee."

I love you. You remember that on the days when I can't tell you in person.

You remember that love and you keep it alive.

Forever,
Your father

James folded the letter and then stood up and walked over to the dresser. He opened the thin black box and looked at the medal inside. They had wanted to put the Bronze Star on him in his casket, but his father had been vehement about James keeping it.

"That is your medal, Son. You keep it front and center to remind you."

He had given both of his children something. Richard had been awarded the medal for saving another's life.

James glanced at the letter, then slipped it underneath the black box.

He studied the star but his thoughts were elsewhere.

They were with his father.

He wondered if his father watched him now. He wondered if his father could read his mind.

I want to be just like you one day.

James knew then and there. There wasn't any question, not anymore.

Part Two

LETTERS FROM TRAINING

Beth

"Excuse me. You're Elizabeth Thompson, right?"

The man with the round face and wide eyes stands between her and the registers at the grocery store. She doesn't recognize the man but instantly assesses that he's probably not military and probably not media.

Hopefully not media.

"I'm Stan Maddox. Hi. My son is planning on going into the army. He just graduated from high school. His name is Vince—a good kid, too—and he was inspired, like all of us, really, by the story of James. You are his mother, right?"

She nods and tries to reassure him with a polite smile.

"We saw that piece on the news last Christmas. Amazing story. I'm so sorry."

"Thank you."

While Beth was used to this, the *Hey, are you James*

Thompson's mother? comments, she was never used to the *I'm sorry* affirmations.

It always reminded her of someone saying "I'm sorry for your loss."

She wanted to say that he wasn't lost. But that's exactly what James was.

"My son saw that interview and said that's what he wanted to do. He wanted to be a hero like James. He wanted to battle those evil people overseas. He wanted to fight for this country."

"When does he leave?"

"He leaves for Fort Benning this fall."

"That's where James went."

"We know."

For some reason Beth felt compelled to say, "Do you know what I told James shortly after he was there? Or actually, what I wrote to him? Something I remember my husband telling me years ago. He said that the most difficult part of basic training wasn't the physical aspect or the mental aspect, but the overall change. Dealing with being scrutinized and having your entire way of life vanish, along with dealing with fifty-something unique personalities are the hardest parts. Make sure your son finds a few good friends to rely on, because he's going to feel completely alone at times."

"Those are good words to know—thank you," Stan says. "Do you mind me asking . . ."

"It's okay," she says.

"Have you heard anything new?"

"No. Not yet."

"We're believers, you know. And we're praying for you guys. For James. And for all of you."

"Thank you."

Her words are sincere because she knows how valuable prayers can be.

The man shakes his head and seems to think whether he should ask anything else, then awkwardly walks away. Beth pushes her half-full grocery cart toward the checkout counter, thinking with fondness about the place she hasn't thought about for a while:

Fort Benning.

It seems like a hundred years ago. And yesterday.

———

There is something lost in this era of e-mail. Some might call her old-fashioned, she knows, but reading words on a computer screen doesn't compare to the experience of opening a letter. Knowing that the handwritten words and carefully creased pages were slipped inside an envelope to travel hundreds or even thousands of miles makes their reception all the more wonderful. Tangible mail is so much more special than the static ping of an arriving e-mail. Seeing a letter in its sometimes messy glory makes it feel like the person who sent it is there, like it's a small version of them they mailed halfway around the world.

On a slow burn of a summer day, the house is quiet after a visit to the local pool. Beth knows enough to stay out of the sun, but even being in the shade on a hot day like today drains the life out of her. She stays inside. She knows that Emily is asleep on the couch, the soft hum of the television in the family room providing the same function that the noise of a fan might. Yet even in the silence of her air-conditioned room, she feels restless. It's the same soft hum that seems to have been there ever since Emily came back.

You know it's been there longer. You know it's been there ever since you heard the news about James.

It doesn't help that friends and family members are openly sharing their doubt. It doesn't help that strangers come up to her with words of "encouragement." It doesn't help that this is a life she can't take off and put in the washing machine.

Eventually Beth finds herself sitting in her walk-in closet that has plenty of room for two adults and seems ridiculous for one. She's opened one of several shoeboxes, yet instead of opening the Nordstrom box to find a pair of shoes, she pulls out a carefully organized set of letters.

To a casual onlooker, shoeboxes would make sense in a closet. Yet not even Emily knows that these boxes store letters. They date back from the time Richard first went off to training and continue through James's last letter.

The box she has pulled out has the first set of letters from James.

E-mails can easily be lost. All with an errant click of a mouse or a press of a button.

To discard a letter, you have to physically throw it away, something she's been unable to do ever since getting that first letter from Richard back in 1984, the same year he proposed.

She sees her son's meticulous handwriting. Controlled and never careless, just like his personality. Beth doesn't know if handwriting can show a person's heart and soul, but it certainly seems to for James.

The very first letter he sent her is at the top. This is one that she opens often. It still surprises her the way it did years ago. In the large and quiet house on a sleepy June afternoon, Beth opens the letter dated September 24, 2006.

Soon she begins unfolding letter after letter.

They are as powerful as a picture slideshow or a home movie. Perhaps even more.

Pictures and film can show faces and smiles and experiences, but they don't always show sentiment.

Words are different. Words reach the soul.

She has almost memorized these letters, yet she continues to read them to hear from James and to keep believing.

She can hear him speaking as she reads the words.

They are beautiful, just as he is.

September 24, 2006

Dear Mom:

I thought I'd be a little more nervous about the nine weeks ahead of me, but I'm not. I felt more nervous in the hours leading up to saying good-bye. I wasn't sure how the party and the farewells would go. Guess I was afraid of getting too emotional. Good thing I got out right before tears showed up!

I'm writing this on the bus headed to Fort Benning. I'm still stunned at how many showed up at the party. Did you pay people to come or something? I know—a lot of it is because of Dad. I think that if it had just been the three of us, I would have felt his absence. But the thirty-plus people who came to say good-bye more than compensated for Dad not being able to.

I wanted to write to thank you. Not for the party—I mean, yes, I want to thank you for that, and I want to thank you for the gift. But I really want to thank you for something else.

I want to thank you for being a really good mother. I could say words like "kind" and "loving" and all that, and you're all of those. But I just think you're an awesome mom. I admire how strong you are, around Emily and me, around others. I can't imagine having another mother. You've always been there for me, and I know even now you always will be. It's comforting knowing that. I'm sure I'm going to have to remind myself of that a lot over the next couple of months.

Thank you for never once trying to convince me not to do this. I know the words you said before I left—I will remember them always, Mom. But I'm not going anywhere. Not yet. Right now, I'm just going to get beat up and then strengthened—physically and mentally. I'm ready, but I'm sure I'll be even readier after graduation.

I don't know how often I'll be able to be in touch, but my promise to you is that I'll keep the tradition Dad started when the two of you were together. I just ask that you write me back as often as possible. It'll be nice to hear a voice from back home. I'll add the accent myself.

I love you. Send my love to Emily—this letter is as much for her as it is for you (not that she'll appreciate it!). Will write and call again soon.

James

October 1, 2006

Dear Mom:

I can't write long—we only get an hour or not even that of personal time every evening—but wanted to thank you for your letter. It means a lot. It's nice to hear those words and to remember them throughout the day. When I can.

I gotta tell you—it sure would be easier e-mailing. But I know you hate e-mail and the Web and all that. I know that was part of our deal.

Training has been tough, I won't kid you. But I'm doing well. The first couple of days with the reception battalion went on forever with waiting around and paperwork. You should see me now. Man do I have an ugly head with my hair gone. Waiting around was hard because I had no idea what—and when—something was going to finally start happening.

So let me share how God works in great ways.

On day five here, I was emotionally gone. I don't know—I thought I'd be stronger but it was just getting to me. Getting to my head. I was really going to break down. But this guy named Carter who's from Texas took me under his wing and helped me out. I almost think he's a guardian angel, though I don't think guardian angels use that kind of language and talk about girls that way.

Things are better. It's strange—you go eighteen years

and then suddenly your whole life changes. Like that. Not in a bad way. I know what they're doing and why they're doing it and I keep that in the back of my mind. I also think of Dad, of you guys, of the people back in our neighborhood and in our church.

I think about all of you when things start getting too heavy.

I'm not here to follow in Dads footsteps. I'm here to serve all of you and to serve this country.

Day by day I'm beginning to understand that a little more.

It fills me with pride even when the muscles are aching and the mind is close to breaking.

That's all I can say for now. I'm going to be learning soon how to shoot an M16. Hopefully I'll qualify the first time.

Look forward to talking to you soon and hearing your voice.

Love you,
James

Beth stops reading the letters and puts them back in order.

She remembers the words she wrote after one of these early letters. She shared a passage from Romans that was meant to encourage. She could still recite it word for word: *We also glory in tribulations, knowing that tribulation produces perseverance; and perseverance, character; and character, hope.*

Beth had told James to continue to persevere and hope. That had been early on during his time at Fort Benning.

I need to do the same. I must do the same. I must remain hopeful.

———

"This must be your little sister," the raspy voice says.

"Behave, Murphy. You don't want to mess with Emily."

Beth shuts the door of the van and walks around the passenger side, noticing Emily's unamused glance through the open window. When she gets behind the wheel of the familiar vehicle, she can hear the man in the back already probing Emily for information.

"I bring Murphy to Mountain Home every Tuesday," Beth says.

She had woken Emily up and urged her to come with her this morning. At first, Emily had asked if this was like one of those Angel Tree things they'd done together around Christmastime. Beth hadn't said what they were going to do, but the moment they arrived at the Mountain Home VA Medical Center to switch vehicles, Emily knew.

"Why do you want me to come?"

"To keep me company," Beth had replied.

But Murphy was company enough.

Beth wanted Emily to participate in this weekly ritual to understand just a little more. A little more about service, about veterans, about a part of the military that she could never learn from her father.

As she starts up the car, she can smell the odor filling the van. It's one of the bitter realities of life. Age has a scent, whether it's the top of a baby's head or the deeply etched wrinkles on a man's hands.

"Tell Emily a little about yourself, Murphy," Beth says.

"I'm dying, how 'bout that?"

Emily glances over and gives her the *Get me out of here* look.

"Maybe a little something about you. A little something lighter."

"Lighter, huh? I was married once. For a couple of days. But turns out she couldn't speak English and didn't quite know what she was getting herself into. Plus, the guy who married us wasn't exactly legit."

"Murphy served in the Korean War, didn't you?"

"Ever heard of that one?"

"Korea?" Emily says, not trying to hide her amusement. "Is that a country or a type of illness?"

The cackle fills the van. "She's got your sense of humor, huh? Korea is the unsexy war. Even Vietnam got all them movies made about it. I think it's better being known for something than nothing."

He's in one of his feisty moods today.

"You got a chance to go back to Korea a couple of years ago, didn't you?"

The eighty-four-year-old man lets out a curse as naturally as he might sneeze. "They tried to make it into an Alaskan cruise. I think I gained ten pounds going back to Korea. And I was surrounded by a bunch of old people. It was embarrassing."

Beth and Emily both laugh.

"Murphy, do you know that Emily here goes to Tennessee?"

This, of course, is the absolute wrong thing to say. It prompts the wrath of Murphy, a longtime Vols fan who doesn't quite appreciate the way the team has gone.

"That last coach of ours—he set us back a good decade."

"I'm sorry," Emily says. "I can't comment on the team. I'm just a cheerleader."

Murphy lets out a good-natured curse. "If you're a cheerleader, I'm a priest."

"What? I don't have the look of a cheerleader?"

"You have more important things to do," Murphy replies. "Right?"

"How are you feeling today?" Beth asks, trying to steer the conversation away from what might turn into bickering.

"How do you feel when you're dying? I don't know. They told me I was going to die in Korea when I got shot. But I don't know."

"Maybe the good Lord has still got some plans for you."

"Sure doesn't feel like it," Murphy says, a spotted relic of a hand wiping his mouth for a minute. "If He does I wish He'd get on with it."

When they arrive at the hospital and Beth goes around to get his wheelchair, she can see him extending a hand to Emily.

"Never get old, pretty lady," he says. "There's nothing good about age except memories. And those just get you down."

"Well, now you even have me depressed," Emily says, smiling. "Come on. We don't want you to be late."

"Amazing how I have to hurry just to sit in some room and wait on a doctor to come."

"Those doctors know what's best for you," Beth says.

The bony figure with the oversized shirt and pants

lets out a sound that resembles an old man's version of "Whatever."

With attitude, of course.

———

"What's wrong with him?" Emily asks shortly after they watch Murphy wheel himself away.

"He must not have had his V8 this morning."

"No, I mean, what's he suffering from?"

"Pancreatitis. He says it's from years of drinking. He blames the war, and he blames the government for sending him to the war. Ultimately he blames God, yet in the same breath says there is no God."

"Great attitude."

"It's sad. He's a good man. He's just alone, in a lot of pain, having to deal with this by himself."

"That's why you do this?"

"He knows our story, Em. The one thing is he can't complain too much around me. He can't have this woe-is-me attitude because he knows I'll call him on the carpet. He's knows where we've been."

"Was he ever married? Really?"

"He was pulling your leg. At least I think he was with that story. His wife died years ago. He has some kids and grandkids but they don't live close by."

"So he's sorta adopted you?" Emily asks.

"He served in the army and he respects the sacrifice

and the service that your father and James gave. He talks about James as if he's still alive."

"Really?"

"Yeah. I don't know why, of all people, Murphy is one of the few who still believe."

"He could be a bit senile."

"No. He might be a lot of things, but he's as sharp as anybody. He's a realist, too. But he believes in the power of the military. He knows the strength of the men and women serving."

"That doesn't mean he should believe that James is alive."

"Emily, don't."

"Don't say the obvious?"

"That's not fair."

"Not fair?" Emily asks. "Not fair to who? To you?"

"That's not fair to James."

"To James? Mom, please."

They drive in silence for a long time, Beth trying to figure out what to say, trying to make sure she doesn't widen the already growing gap.

"Why is hope a bad thing?" she finally says to her daughter.

"I'm not saying it is. But why is letting go such a bad thing, either? I've done it and it's worked for me."

She wants to hold back and probably should, but

her mouth and her tongue already move faster than the speed limit.

"Well then, I'm really sorry that it's worked out so well for you."

———

It's nice to know that Beth isn't the only fool to still believe that James is alive.

Love has the ability to do that. To suspend all belief. To cling to hope, to persevere.

Even when the signs and reason tell you not to.

Yet even though Beth refuses to give up, she wonders if Britt maybe should.

How can I even think such a thing?

She pauses for a moment as she turns off the car. The modest driveway in front of the modest house is a pale representation of the anything-but-modest love held inside of it. Beth opens the door and feels the coating of humidity cover her instantly. She notices the lawn that needs cutting, flowers that desperately need water.

A home needs a family to fill it. All members of a family.

It's one thing for Beth to keep hoping, but Britt's hope means she'll never move on, never be able to live a normal life.

They barely had enough time to say their wedding vows, much less start a family.

They found out they were expecting in February, a couple of months before James went to Afghanistan. It was bittersweet news, of course, knowing the possibilities that followed in the father's footsteps. James had told her he didn't want to know what they were having, not until he was holding the baby in his hands for the first time. Because of this Britt had decided to be surprised along with him.

James went missing in August, three months before Britt found out that they were indeed having what he had hoped: a son.

Beth knocks and sees the beautiful redhead at the door. Her smile is weighted, certainly different from the smile on her wedding day three years ago.

No matter how many times I come to this door, the reality will always travel with me like some mangled suitcase of despair. I shouldn't be here. Someone else should be.

"How are you?" she asks as they hug.

"Hanging in there," Britt says.

Beth is going to ask what's wrong, since Britt normally doesn't answer this way, at least not right away and in this tone. Then she remembers when she hears the little footsteps on the floor and the jangle of a collar.

The black and tan puffball runs toward her and then back and around. Britt bends down and scoops him up.

"Come on, Bailey."

It takes them only a minute to find the little puddle Bailey left behind.

"He's not quite used to company yet."

"He just likes seeing me. Don't you? Here—I'll get it."

"No, it's fine, really."

"It's barely a few drops," Beth says. "Please."

"Can you picture James's reaction to this dog?"

Beth laughs as she gets some paper towels. "I'd love to see that."

"He always wanted a big dog."

"When he comes back, he can get one."

The sound of other footsteps and a joyful shout come as Richie greets his grandma. Beth scoops him up.

"Who needs a big dog when you have a big man of the house?" Beth says. "He's sure growing. You must be feeding him something I don't know about."

"I follow strict rules. I'm an army wife, remember."

Britt looks as trim and vibrant as she did on her wedding day. Perhaps a bit too trim, in fact. She pets the dog and kisses it as Beth holds Richie.

"How's the lady of the house doing?"

"Keeping busy with my little guy and our new pet."

The nine-week-old puppy has been with Britt for only a few weeks. It seems to still be getting used to its feet, bouncing around and sniffing Beth.

"You taking care of yourself?"

"I already have several women asking me that daily at work," Britt says, smiling.

"How is work?"

"It's good. It takes my mind off things. Sometimes."

Along with babysitting for Britt on weekday mornings, Beth visits her daughter-in-law once a week. When Richie was first born, Beth stayed over many nights. As he's grown older, this is the tradition that remained. The weekly visit feels as natural and vital as that first cup of coffee in the morning.

For a while, they talk about Richie. Beth gives her a weekly update, telling Britt about different things he's done or said or funny stories. It's a nice thing to have something to talk about besides James. Sometimes the same conversation with the same questions becomes more and more draining.

Life can and should be about more than James. We are family now, friends, and it's important to create new memories as that.

James and Britt bought the house shortly before getting married in June of 2008. Just as with any couple, the future seemed as bright and wide open as the sky above.

Life can be deceptive like that.

"So Emily couldn't come?"

"She had to work at O'Malley's."

"How does she like it?"

"It's okay. I think some of the guys she has to serve irritate her. But most of them are the big tippers so she has to live with it."

"They have great food. A bit pricey. Not that I've been there since James and I went last."

It's only been a year since she graduated from East Tennessee State with a degree in nursing. Though Britt hasn't ever said so, Beth likes to think that the degree comes from wanting to help people in need just like her husband is doing.

Not everybody needs a gun to help people.

That was something Richard had said years ago to encourage Beth when he was off at war.

It was a thought she carried around like a license and a key.

For a while, Britt shares about her job at the hospital, about the part-time hours that feel like they're full-time, and how she's adjusting to taking care of a puppy now along with a toddler.

"How is Emily doing?"

"With school?"

"With things."

It's nice to hear Richie and Bailey playing on the floor in the kitchen. Beth knows that this house would have been very different, very quiet, had they not been blessed with Richie nineteen months ago.

"Sometimes it's hard to know beneath her endless sarcasm," Beth says. "She says she's 'moved on.'"

For a moment, Britt doesn't say anything.

"And I think that's great, even if I don't exactly believe her. She takes after her father. She's tough that way."

"And you're not?"

"I'm different. No. I think she's a lot like Richard—a realist. I'm stubborn but I'm also sentimental."

"Believing that James is alive isn't sentimental."

Beth nods. She doesn't want to discount anything that Britt says. "It's amazing how certain traits in parents show up in different ways in their children."

"James is a lot like you."

"They both are, yet for half their lives they've only known me. So of course it's easy for them to be influenced by me."

"He sees the world through your eyes."

"I think Emily does the same through her father's eyes. Sometimes something she says or does reminds me of him and it will be this bittersweet moment . . . that is ultimately too painful to dwell on."

"I wish I could have known him."

She takes Britt's hand and squeezes it. "I wish you could have known—that you could *know* James better."

"I believe I will. I truly do." Britt smiles, but a bit sadly.

A squeal from the kitchen interrupts them. They both go to find Richie on his hands and knees playing with Bailey's food.

As she watches Britt prevent Richie from eating the dog food by picking him up, Beth wants to tell her daughter-in-law she always believed that even though Richard was diagnosed with cancer, he would never leave them. Or perhaps he would leave them when the children were older and married and had moved on. But no—this had been her belief and she was wrong.

God had another plan.

That wonderful saying about God and His "plans."

"I know what other people think," Britt says. "But I still believe he's out there. I mean—it felt like we married and then boom, he was in Afghanistan."

"He was. Do you know that when James was born, we'd only been married a year?"

"How old were you?"

"I was barely twenty-one. A couple years younger than you two."

"Wow," Britt says. "I felt like we married young."

"You did. A lot of our friends married a lot later than we did. But Richard always had a grand plan: marriage, army, children."

"Sounds like James."

Beth reaches over and again takes her daughter-in-law's soft hand. "The master plan has a way of changing, doesn't it?"

"Yes it does."

"Do you remember the first time James brought you over to our house? Do you want to know something?"

"What is it?"

"I can't believe I never told you this," Beth says. "When we were in the kitchen and you were talking to Emily, James whispered to me that he was going to marry you."

"He told me."

"Yes, but did he ever tell you what I said?"

Britt shakes her head, smiling. "Do I want to know?"

"I said not to rush. I told him that you shouldn't rush marriage, that you have to be certain. It wasn't anything against you. It was just that he was in high school, with plans of going into the army. I always thought, *Just wait. Just wait because I know that road for the wife.* I know how difficult it can be."

"What did he say to that?"

"He said that you never know how much time you have in this life. Then he said, looking into the room where you were, that he wasn't going to take any time for granted. Not with someone like you. James said that once you know, you know, and then you fight to keep knowing. Even if you have to fight the rest of your life."

For a moment, the young woman across from her

seems lost. The freckles drizzled across her nose are barely visible under the soft glow of the kitchen light. Richie is making grunting noises as she holds him.

"What'd he mean by that?"

"You know, at the time I didn't know. He was just eighteen. But over the years I've come to believe that he meant that if you find something in this life that you believe in and love, you need to embrace that thing and then fight to keep believing and loving it."

"He really said that?"

"My teen boy," Beth says. "And that's when I knew. I knew that this beautiful little redheaded girl he brought to my door had suddenly turned him into Shakespeare, romantic and all."

The tears no longer hide in the edges of Britt's eyes. She silently wipes her cheeks.

"Wherever he is, James is fighting. He's fighting to be back here, standing where I'm standing, holding Richie in his arms, and looking at you and laughing and loving."

Britt nods and sighs and wipes away more tears.

"I wish he knew that he has a son to hold."

"I think he knows. Maybe deep down, in some strange and untold way, God whispered to him that you guys had a son."

"It's hard to think that—to think that he's alive and hurting or that he's dead."

"I know," Beth says.

"Am I being selfish asking God to keep him alive?"

"Absolutely not. My dear, you're just being practical."

"I don't know."

"I still don't know why God took Richard so early. And there are times, God knows, that I grow resentful and angry. But that's the beauty of prayer. We can talk to God and know that He will hear us. He's heard a lot from me. He knows. He knows and I have to believe that He cares."

"You, resentful and angry? Please."

"I'm a woman," Beth says. "I know how to put on a pretty face and hide the wrinkles well."

Before leaving the house just after sunset, the two women do what they always do.

Pray.

It's still something that Beth can't fully fathom. This ability to come before the Maker of heaven and the stars and mankind to petition Him. This opportunity to ask.

Not every prayer is answered, and Beth knows this the hard way.

Yet some are.

And everything, every single thing, is part of His plan.

If she didn't believe this, she would break down and would never, ever, *ever* move on.

Being able to share a little of this with her daughter-in-law is a gift.

Even if the gift she shares comes wrapped in pain.

June 24, 2011

Dear James,

If only you could see Britt. She loves you more today than on the day you two married. I can see it in her eyes, can hear it in her words, can feel it when I hold her hand.

Sometimes it's good to be reminded—even by your mother—that you are missed and you are loved. I'm not the only one who misses you.

Last night I had this dream of walking up to your house and opening the door and seeing you standing there with Richie. You handed him to me and I could see stains on your shirt—something green and messy. It was quite the vivid dream. It probably didn't help that not only did I see Britt and Richie last night, but I was going through old photo albums.

You always looked like a baby version of your father. The shape of his face and the twinkle in that smile.

Richie has that same shine about him.

I know what an amazing father you'll be one day, just as your father was. Sometimes these dreams that come—sometimes I feel they're gifts. Not premonitions or visions but gifts of what could be. When I woke up last night, I prayed that a dream like this could one day be reality.

I told God I'd splatter you with green goop myself.

Anything to bring you home.

Anything to keep you safe.

I love you and I still fight for you. God hears these prayers, I know He does. And so I know He watches over you.

Mom

———

The enemy waits and watches, wanting to destroy any semblance of hope, wanting to dismantle any series of prayers.

As Beth watches the news, a small part of her gets flattened. Like the tread of tires in soft mud, the marks are imprinted and won't go away any time soon.

Beth likes this particular anchor on NBC. She likes the integrity and grace with which he handles issues, like the one he reports about today. Another wave of deadly violence in Afghanistan, another list of casualties. One report details how the soldiers die; another then quickly goes into the seemingly endless war that the locals and Americans are getting tired of.

She turns off the news and sits on the edge of her couch.

Dear Father, be with those families today. Give them extra strength to make it through their loss. Please help them come together and come closer to You.

A name and a number on television aren't just a name and a number to her. She is going to ask a friend to look up those families so she can send them a card. A mother of an MIA to a mother of a KIA. She knows she has a right to send a card and share her condolences. Yet Beth still admits that she doesn't know what they're going through. Not yet.

Is it getting worse or is it just me?

She thinks of the key ring with the carved seed on it, the one she gave to James some time ago. She is reminded of the gift from a friend and what that tiny seed stands for.

Faith.

It was given to her shortly after James was deployed to Iraq that first time. Ironically, the person who gave it to her, who told her never to give up believing, was Josie. The same person who was encouraging her to let go of James now.

I wonder where that key ring is today. I wonder if whoever took James took that from him.

The news is a reminder for her to keep believing even amid the tragedy. Every day, if she carefully waits for it, there will be some kind of bad news coming out of Afghanistan. Yet she has to remind herself why the soldiers are there and what they stand for.

As she finds her car keys to head out of the house, Beth remembers what she told James just before his graduation day.

James

They spoke in controlled and deliberate unison, strong and emphatic and concise.

"I am the infantry," they called out. "I am my country's strength in war, her deterrent in peace. I am the heart of the fight—wherever, whenever. I carry America's faith and honor against her enemies. I am the queen of battle."

The words were ones James knew by heart simply because they resided there.

"I am what my country expects me to be: the best-trained soldier in the world. In the race for victory, I am swift, determined, and courageous, armed with a fierce will to win."

They weren't nameless, faceless figures in full dress

standing at attention on this cold winter day. Every one of them was watched over with love by the spectators who stood before them.

"Never will I fail my country's trust. Always I fight on—through the foe, to the objective, to triumph over all. If necessary, I fight to my death."

The men around James would always be his brothers. They had all arrived at Fort Benning as boys. And they were all leaving as more than men.

"By my steadfast courage, I have won two hundred years of freedom. I yield not—to weakness, to hunger, to cowardice, to fatigue, to superior odds. For I am mentally tough, physically strong, and morally straight."

They were now following in great and mighty footsteps.

"I forsake not—my country, my mission, my comrades, my sacred duty."

They were now shadowed by legends and ready to step out in the sun.

"I am relentless. I am always there, now and forever."

They were and would always carry this designation.

"I am the infantry! Follow me!"

The designation as infantrymen.

This was what it felt like to have brothers. Guys who could wrestle you down on the ground and shove your face into the dirt until you hollered in submission. Guys who could mock you about the girl back home and the way you talked about her all the time. Guys who could stand alongside you and be willing to step in front of you to take a bullet one day.

Brothers.

James had always wondered what it would be like. Boot camp had been a series of out-of-body experiences. The father he barely knew was his drill instructor. The brothers he never had were his teammates.

James thought of this as he stood in the row listening and sounding off and standing straight.

The guys standing around him—they weren't guys to just hang out with. They weren't video-playing buddies. They weren't snowboarding buddies. These guys were of a different fabric and caliber.

This was the Turning Blue ceremony for them, the day before they officially graduated.

It was a simple ceremony, yet the significance could not be fully weighed or articulated by James, his mother, or his sister.

At the end of the ceremony, loved ones were given the opportunity to attach a blue infantry cord to their class A uniforms.

James knew who would have done it had he been there.

But someone else would do it. Someone just as strong and just as proud.

The blue cord distinguished the infantrymen from the

rest of the army and symbolized entry into the brotherhood of infantrymen. This blue cord linked all of them to every infantryman who ever served and would ever serve.

His mother came flanked by Emily and Britt to attach the blue braid to the right lapel so that it encircled his shoulder.

Proud tears filled her eyes.

"Where did my boy go?" she asked him.

He smiled at her but didn't reply. He helped her attach the cord, bending his knees so she could easily do it. After it was on, they posed for several pictures, then she gave him a big hug.

"He's smiling down on you, James," she whispered in his ear.

He almost let the tears come, but he fought them off.

A sergeant came up to congratulate James. He smiled at his mom, charming her with an air of civility James hadn't seen for fourteen weeks.

"They were good boys," the sergeant said. "When they get home, they'll know how to clean their rooms and make their beds."

It was strange to have forgotten the simplicities of life. Going out to dinner and laughing about familiar incidents and people. The evening gave James the luxury of being with Britt and his mom and sister. Graduation would be tomorrow.

The small things mattered in a big way. He could say that now after getting through this first part and seeing the world in a new light. Small things like eating at Red Lobster and scarfing down six warm cheddar biscuits before his steak and lobster came. Small things like sitting next to Britt in the booth and feeling her body always touching his, even when they got their food. Small things like joking with Emily about the guy she was dating and still finding a way to push all her buttons.

His sides hurt from laughing and his mouth was sore from smiling.

It was nice to get a little break and celebrate.

After saying good-bye to Britt and Emily, Beth followed him back away from the car so she could talk with him. It was colder and windy and her light jacket didn't seem warm enough.

"You better get back in the car," he said.

"I will. I just need to say something."

"Oh, no. Here it comes."

"Stop," she said playfully. "I just want you to know something. And I could wait but I know better than to wait on things like this. You should say them in the moment. I learned that the hard way when it came to your father."

He stood waiting for his mother to continue. He could see the tears in her eyes even though it was dark out and the faint light from the streetlamp was the only thing that allowed them to see.

She continued. "I want you to know how proud I am to see you in that uniform. Not because your father was in that uniform. That delights me and I know it delights your father too. But I want you to know something Richard once told me with unabashed pride. He said that only about one percent of the U.S. population ever gets to wear the military uniform. That means you are in that rare one percent and you will always be, whatever happens from this day forward."

James wasn't sure what to say, so he answered with a nod.

"You're still my baby and you always will be, you understand? That no matter *what* uniform you're wearing, you're my little boy. So that means you need to take care of yourself, understand that? You need to come home safe."

"Of course."

She gave him a hug and then told him to get a good night's rest. They would see him tomorrow at graduation and the subsequent parties to follow.

James watched his mother get swallowed by the darkness as she went to the parking lot. He stood and thought about her words and then thought about the day.

It had been an exceptional day.

But his story—*this* story—had just begun.

DECEMBER 24, 2006

He held her hand in silence, the drive from her parents' house a short fifteen minutes. Yet the silence made the passing miles feel longer.

"You okay?" Britt asked.

"Yeah, sure."

"Then what's wrong?"

"Nothing."

"Where'd you go? After opening presents?"

"Nowhere."

Britt usually would leave things alone but she didn't seem as if she was going to tonight. Maybe because it was Christmas Eve and this was one of those times when his reticence simply didn't belong.

"What's going on, James?"

"Nothing. Really."

"You've been distant all night."

"I've been here."

"But your mind is somewhere else. You seem worried. Is it because you're leaving soon?"

"No." His answer was a bit too abrupt, and he squeezed her hand right after uttering it. "I'm sorry. But that's not it."

"It would be okay if it was."

"But it's not. Really."

He knew what was coming and he knew it shouldn't be preceded by an argument. That was the last thing he wanted. But his mind and his gut and his heart all stormed inside.

There's no training for this. None at all.

He looked over at her in the dim light of the truck.

She's so beautiful. I don't want to leave her, even though I'm going to very soon.

"James?"

"Yeah."

"Why is it so much easier for you to write what you feel rather than say it in person?"

"I don't know. It just is."

"You can say anything to me. You don't have to worry."

"I'm not worried."

"Then what is it?"

"The words sound different spoken out loud."

"But they aren't."

"Yeah, maybe they aren't. But they just lose their meaning a bit. At least to me, when I say them. And I don't want to do that. I told you how I feel."

"I want to hear you say it."

"Britt, come on."

"Nobody's around. Not now. You can tell me anything."

"I know."

"You don't have to be distant. You don't—you don't have time to be distant."

"I know that."

"James?"

"Just wait until we get home."

"But then your mother and Emily will be there."

"They will leave us alone. I promise."

"You don't know that."

"I asked."

"You're scaring me," Britt said.

"Why?"

"Because. Because it's almost like—I don't know. It's like you're going to break up with me or something."

Girls, he thought as he shook his head. *Some things really don't make any sense in this world.*

"Why would you be spending the night at our house if I wanted to break up?"

"I don't know."

"That would make for a really awkward Christmas morning, wouldn't it?"

"But then I don't get—"

He interrupted her with a "Shhhhh."

Even though they were almost back to his house, the few minutes still felt too long.

Too long and not long enough.

———

The fire crackled and glowed as the scent of Christmas filled the room. James and Britt had turned off the television and they sat on the couch under a blanket.

"I want to give you your present tonight," he said.

She looked at him with genuine surprise. "I thought that's why I was going to spend the night—so we could open them with your mom and sister in the morning."

"I know. This is just something you'll like."

"Really?"

"Oh, don't give me that look," he said. "It's just a letter."

"I like letters," she told him.

But the glow on her face lessened a bit.

"You said it yourself—I say things better in letter form. Maybe I get that from my dad, I don't know. So I wrote you this."

"Are you still going to write to me when you're in Iraq?"

"Mom already made me promise to write to her."

"You can't write both?"

He laughed and nudged her. "Go on, read it."

Her face was lit up in a way no camera or spotlight

could ever effect. She smiled and looked so innocent and cute and adorable and charming and sexy all at the same time.

He would never tell her all of that, at least not yet, but he couldn't help thinking it as he turned on a lamp next to them and she began reading his letter.

Dear Britt:

Hopefully it's Christmas Eve and we're alone and I finally have a chance to tell you some of the things that have been on my mind and heart recently. I'm writing them because that's what I do best. It's better than rambling on or forgetting to finish the sentence. It's better because I don't have to be watched as I open up and bare my soul.

I want to thank you for coming into my life and for chasing after me. Sometimes guys are too dumb to see what's right in front of them. Sometimes guys are too focused on the future and the almighty "plan." Well—I was too dumb and too focused to notice the beautiful and tender girl who seemed to keep coming across my path.

Thanks for not giving up on me. Thank you for wanting to be with me even though you knew what I wanted to do and where I wanted to go.

I want to tell you something that I've hinted at but never really told you before.

I haven't said it because—well, once I say it, you will know.

So I won't say it. I will write it.

It didn't take me a summer, Britt. It didn't take basic training and writing back and forth, nor did it take a holiday together.

I knew on that first date we went on.

I knew that I wanted to spend the rest of my life with you.

What I didn't know was what I was supposed to do with that information. I held it close. I tried not to reveal it because I wasn't sure how you felt.

I remember leaving your house that night and thinking to myself, I want to marry that girl. She's the one.

There are many ways a man can ask the woman he loves to marry him. But to me, the thing that matters is not the how. It's the why.

Britt stopped reading and hugged him, the tears glistening on her face.

"Did you finish it?" James asked.

"No, not yet, but I just wanted to—"

He kissed her for what felt like a second and an eternity, then he whispered for her to keep reading.

And this is the why.

I believe you are strong. Deep down, you are solid and are that rock I'll be able to lean on.

You're not outspoken or tough or abrasive. Yours is a quiet strength.

I believe that is what I need—what we need—in order to make this work.

I have told you what I think of you and why I love

being with you—why I love you. You make me feel alive.
You are everything that is soft and tender and good about
this world. Your faith makes me want to strengthen
mine. Your love makes me want to never leave your side.

So I ask you a question and will follow it with a
promise.

Will you marry me, Britt Alexander?

Will you complete a dream come true and give all of
yourself to me, even if I'm not there?

Will you let me spend the rest of my life loving you?

I promise you that regardless of what happens and
where I am, I will never stop loving you. Never.

I'll be by your side, even when I'm far away and we
can't talk or write.

I will try my best if you let me.

James

As she put down the letter and looked at him, James wiped the tears off her cheeks.

"I disappeared tonight because I let your father read that letter."

Britt laughed and continued to wipe the tears away. "What did he say?"

"Believe it or not, he even shed a tear."

"Yes, James. Yes."

"You believe me?"

"I will stand by your side whatever happens and wherever you go. Yes. Yes."

He moved and pulled a little box from underneath the couch.

"In that case, you might want to see this. It's just a little something I picked up. It's nothing much."

One of the things Britt said she liked about him was his sarcasm. Especially in this case.

Part Three

LETTERS FROM IRAQ

Beth

The doorbell rings in the sanctuary of her dreams, a bell choir of children playing "Amazing Grace" as she sits in the empty pew and empty church. It takes a few rings for Beth to open her eyes and realize that it's an actual doorbell.

She sits up in bed, not breathing, eyes wide open and fearful, her body numb.

It is two thirty in the morning.

James.

She knows and she doesn't need to go downstairs to find out. She can see the suit of the man standing there without opening the door. She can hear the words before they are uttered. She can feel the hard, cold floor without having to be there to collapse against it.

Her hands shake.

The doorbell rings again, demanding that she get up, daring her to go downstairs.

The walk from her bed to the doorway is eternal.

I walked these same steps as I went to him as a baby, when he cried the ragged cry of a newborn.

She makes it past his room, then past Emily's room.

She notices the open door and then turns on the light.

Emily isn't there.

She sighs and forces herself not to cry, not yet, not now.

It's about time I know. It's about time I finally hear.

The familiar cracks of the stairs. The glow of the light behind her. The blare of the doorbell never sounding so hellish or hateful.

She doesn't need to turn on the porch light. It's already on.

Guess she won't have to leave it on anymore.

Beth unlocks the door and then opens it.

The same door we brought him through after he was born, the same door we walked through hand in hand after Richard died, the same door I stood at to hug him and kiss him good-bye before he left for the last time.

She opens the door. The man is there and she can barely bring herself to look at him.

Her eyes are already full. Her heart and her soul already empty.

"I am Captain . . ." He starts to speak, though she

doesn't hear his name or company name or battalion number.

She's already weeping.

"Are you Mrs. Beth Thompson? Are you the mother of Sergeant James Nathaniel Thompson?"

She always thought she would be stronger, but she is a mess as her shaking hands cover her face. She tries to speak, to say something, to respond with dignity and strength, to honor the memory of James.

"Yes," she says somehow.

"The secretary of the army has asked me to express his deep regret that your son, James, was killed in action in—"

The rest of the sentence isn't uttered, or is mumbled.

"What? How? When?"

"The secretary extends his deepest sympathy to you and your family for your tragic loss."

She wipes her eyes and moves toward the man in front of her.

"How did he die? When? I want to know answers. Tell me. I've been waiting to hear for two years, so tell me now. I need to know."

Then she looks and sees his face.

It's Richard.

He looks just as he did when they married.

"Sweetie," he says, taking her shaking and wet hands.

"No. No no no—this isn't—Richard?"

"It's okay."

"No. Tell me—what? What is happening?"

Her husband is standing there in jeans and a Tennessee Vols shirt, smiling.

"We didn't live here when James was born," he tells her. "You're dreaming."

"I'm what?"

Richard nods, smiling, still holding her hands. "You're dreaming."

"Then . . ."

She hears his laugh as she opens her eyes.

It's only 1:14. There is no doorbell ringing.

Beth moves her hand over her heart and can feel it running a marathon. That's what it has felt like, day after day, night after night. Running to believe. Running to let go. Running to find out the truth. Running away from the truth.

"Lord, please hear my cry," she says. "Please give me an answer. Please, Lord, I beg of You."

Her memory goes to the day the soldier came knocking to tell her that James was missing. Yet she buries it, knowing that is one of those memories, the kind she needs to keep at bay. They are enemies of hope and they lie deep in the waters waiting to emerge and do battle.

That's the way the enemy fights best.

James

James ran through a desert with the full moon trailing him. He could hear only his breath, the quick haggard breathing from running miles. He had dumped everything he could but still carried thirty or forty pounds of gear on him, in pockets and on his belt and around his neck. His heart burned, his legs throbbed, his mind focused on one thing.

Escape.

They cannot kill me. They won't kill me. I won't let them. I won't do that to my mom.

She filled his mind and he knew he needed to be safe. He didn't want to leave her alone. God wouldn't let that happen to his mom.

He ascended a hill and slowed down a bit.

A gunshot sounded from behind him.

James saw a small light and knew that was where he was supposed to go.

Yet he was slowing down. It was inevitable. All the training in the world couldn't make him invincible.

He turned for a moment. Just a single moment.

Something passed through him. Through his side.

There was no choice but to fall.

No no no, I'm not dying, not over here, not like this.

He shouted but the night wind sucked it in.

"James?"

He could hear footsteps and knew they were coming for him.

The warm oozing of his life flowed all around him.

"James, wake up."

He knew he was going to die like this, alone in a sea of sand.

"James, wake up. It's Mom."

Then he felt by his side and could feel the sheet on his bed. The small light came from outside his bedroom. The footsteps had stopped because they belonged to his mother.

His hand touched his bare chest. No wounds. No holes. No gushing.

"It's okay. You're just having a dream."

He shook his head. "That wasn't a dream."

"It's okay. You're awake now."

James let out a sigh and realized it was three in the morning.

He would be leaving for Iraq tomorrow. Or really today.

"I'm all right," he said.

"You sure?"

"Yeah. Thanks."

His mother stood over his bed the way she had countless times before. Then she kissed him on the forehead and left the room.

For a long time, he stared at the darkness of the ceiling above him, wondering whether that had been just a nightmare caused by nerves.

Or if that had been a vision of what was to come.

April 10, 2007

Dear Mom:

I sit here waiting. Ready and waiting to get on the plane. I'm thinking about the soldiers who have come before me. Those who have put on the uniform, preparing to ship out. Those who have served and died for this country and for the freedoms we stand for.

I think of country boys who didn't know anything—not just about the war they were heading to but about the world in general. I think of guys who did the necessary thing and enlisted. I think of a world that was different then, a world torn apart yet united by forces out of control.

The world is different in so many ways. But terror and evil still exist. They're more confined and more elusive, but they're still terrible and demand a fight.

All those soldiers and all those lost lives.

I think about them and think about the path they paved. The notion of war is romantic, especially the great wars. But the reality of them is tragic.

I've thought of these things before, Mom, but not like this.

I guess knowing that I'm heading over to another country to serve and protect both scares me and fills me with a great and burning pride.

You probably already knew I'd be anxious—you didn't

need to hear me having a nightmare to know I was nervous.

I know that God watches over us and will protect us. He can't protect all of us because of the evil in this world, but I know He is there.

So is Dad.

I hope he's smiling down on me tonight. Smiling with the same pride that's filling me up.

On the eve of D-day, General Eisenhower issued a letter to the troops that ended with these words: "Let us beseech the blessing of Almighty God upon this great and noble undertaking."

God is almighty. I've always believed that.

I also believe that this, too, is a great and noble undertaking.

The time is different now, and the great war deserves to be remembered accordingly.

Yet so do we.

So do we.

I love you and Emily and will write or e-mail as soon as I can.

James

Beth

The unfortunate reality about family, those we're not only blessed to love but sometimes also forced to love, is that sometimes what should be a safe haven turns into a three-ring circus of negativity. Yet today, Beth is ready.

She enters the room ready to rumble, as James would say. She wants to make him proud. Not to mention wanting to show off for Richard.

The smell of the pot roast still lingers. It's been a couple of hours since Sunday lunch at her brother's house. It's both a blessing and a curse living close to relatives. Dan is only fifteen minutes away, so birthday get-togethers still happen.

Sometimes it's better if they don't.

Most of the kids are in the basement playing video games. Beth wants to join them. It's the time of the day when the food is settling just like the people in the chairs and the pontificating begins. As usual, everybody easily assumes their given role: the observer, the cynic, the comic, the instigator.

The latter belongs to a round and wrinkled face barely resembling her. Somewhere underneath the jowls that never stop moving and the eyes that never stop menacing are the genes of family that will never change.

Dan Newman sits at the table talking to whoever will listen to him. Beth sometimes wonders if her brother talks to himself in private, rambling on about whatever opinion he feels everybody else should have. The last dozen times she's been around him, the subject of the war and the army and James have all come up. They've come up but she's retreated each and every time.

So go ahead and have the inevitable fight.

She wants things to be different today. Of course he doesn't know and doesn't care if things are different. But this is a cycle Beth is going to break and she's going to do it today.

"Five more soldiers just died yesterday. Those ragheads did it with another explosion. They don't do anything other than plant them and run away like rats."

"It's amazing how you talk about it as if you understand what it's like to be in their shoes," Beth says as she sits down at the dinner table.

Her brother is wearing a golf shirt even though it's probably been ten years since Dan last golfed. "Aw, I'm just saying. It's a shame."

"What's a shame, Dan?"

It's a shame my son has to serve and maybe die over in a war that you mock every single time I'm around you.

"Those boys need to come back home."

"They're more than just boys out there," Rene says to her husband.

It's a miracle for her to get in a sentence between her husband's rants.

"You know what I mean."

"Is it just today, or do you always have to talk about the war and how much you disdain it?"

Dan moves in his chair, his big body shifting from hanging over one side to the other. He laughs and finishes the last bite of cake.

If he could persuade people he might be a good politician. If he was strong enough in his faith, he could make a good pastor. But Dan is stuck in his little bubble and the Sunday dinner table is his podium and pulpit. We, his family, are forced to hear the same spiel whenever we're gathered together.

"Don't get that way, B."

It wasn't always like this. After James entered the service, the talk was always positive. But sometime between James going MIA and Dan becoming more vocal, the patriotic vibes had shifted to something else.

"What way am I being?"

"I'm just talking."

"You're talking about things you don't have the slightest clue about."

She finds it amazing that she's related to this guy. How can her older brother be dumb and uninformed, like a stereotypical redneck?

"Did something happen?" Rene asks.

"Yeah. A couple of years ago. Remember that? Remember that story?"

"Beth, come on," Dan says.

"No. You come on. You were there. You have no idea what it's like to answer that door and see that man standing there waiting to deliver the news—news that only gives half the answer. You don't know what it's like and never will because all of your children are accounted for."

"I'm not talking about James."

"Then what are you talking about? How can you separate James from the rest of the Afghanistan war?"

"You know your brother," Rene says, nonplussed by Beth's outburst. "He lives in a boxed-in world. The town could be in flames and he'd still ask what we're having for dinner."

"The military doesn't even know how to treat their own," Dan adds. "They took away Burger King and Pizza Hut from them last year. Now, why would they go do something like that?"

"God forbid you take Pizza Hut away," Rene says

in amusement. "You'd go AWOL if you couldn't have your Pizza Hut."

"Just because I'm against the war doesn't mean I'm against James."

"Yes it does," Beth says without thought. "Yes it does."

In two years, she's never said or acted quite like this. But everybody has their breaking point.

There is a seemingly endless silence that's interrupted by Emily saying she's leaving.

"Make sure you come home at a decent time," Beth calls out.

She wonders if Emily heard much of the conversation at the dinner table, then she shares a knowing glance with her brother.

He is silent for the time being.

But there will always be a next time.

Always.

—

"Don't let him get to you."

"I know. I just—I shouldn't have overreacted."

"It sounds like it was about time for someone to say something."

Beth thinks that maybe Britt is right, but still. Even if his skull is thick, Dan is still her brother and she loves him. Despite wanting to strangle him most of the time.

They're walking through an outdoor mall, with Richie, thankfully, content for now in his stroller. Beth gives him another ten or fifteen minutes before he gets antsy and needs to get out. She keeps telling Britt to take her time in one of the stores, to really shop and not just casually browse. But Britt isn't there just yet.

"Maybe your brother misses James just like the rest of us," Britt says. "That's just his unique—um—way of showing it."

"Everything he does is certainly unique. To say the least."

As they walk down the sidewalk, a beat-up car chugs by and seems to greet them with a gurgle. It makes Beth think of something she hasn't thought of for a while.

She can't help but laugh.

"What?"

"Did James ever tell you about the car that he tried to salvage with his uncle Dan?"

Britt shakes her head.

"James might be a lot of things, but a mechanic he is not. Once during high school he tried to be all manly and help get Dan's old Ford truck working. It was quite the science experiment."

"James can't fix anything."

"I know. But he tries, doesn't he? Don't tell him he can't do something. He learned long and hard that summer that there are talents in life that God doesn't bless you with."

"But how in the world did he even try to work on it?"

"He found directions online. Which was mistake number one. One of a thousand." Beth smiles the way she might seeing a friend waving to her in a passing car.

"Is Dan handy?"

"He's good at fixing things. But he's also lazy, and James wanted to do it himself. A bad combo, those two. But you know, they had fun."

"What happened to the truck?"

"It's still there, in back of Dan's house. Rene is always after him to clean it up."

"James just left it there?"

"The engine blew up," Beth says. "I mean, *literally* blew up. Ruined. James came home saying that he decided he wasn't a mechanic. He seemed to have oil on every part of his body. Dan said he'd clean up everything. Which, of course, he never did. But I think they had a lot of fun hanging out together."

"Maybe he's just waiting, the way we all are."

Beth looks at Britt and wonders what she means.

"You know—maybe Dan is waiting for James to come home and finish his job."

The call comes in the middle of the night.

Calls like this are never welcome. Yet they're the quickest to be answered.

The conversation is over in a minute. It takes Beth another few to change clothes and leave.

She doesn't think of telling Emily where she's going. Emily probably didn't even hear the phone call and is still fast asleep. Then again, maybe Emily's not even in her bed. Maybe she stayed late at O'Malley's like most of the servers do after their shifts. That's something Beth doesn't want to deal with now.

First things first.

On the drive, she keeps the radio off and the window shut. The silence helps her focus her mind and pray. She prays during the entire trip. Beth won't even be able to remember later if she prayed out loud or silently. She knows it doesn't matter, not with God.

She gets out of the car and rushes up the sidewalk and into the house. Even though they just saw each other this afternoon, Beth knows a lot can change in a matter of hours.

"Britt? Honey, are you in there?"

The phone call scared her. Britt's tone and her words seemed strange and distant. Nowadays, in this cruel and bitter world, one never knows what might happen next. Beth wasn't going to take a chance. Some people will sit back and let things happen but she spends her days waiting and watching, so when she *can* do something, she's going to.

"Britt, where are you?"

She goes into the bedroom to find her daughter-in-law lying on the bed, eyes swollen and cheeks puffy, a box of Kleenex beside her, Bailey lounging comfortably next to a pillow.

"What is it? What happened? Is Richie okay?"

"Yes, he's fine," Britt says. "He's sleeping. Nothing's wrong. You didn't need to come."

"Then what's wrong with you?"

For a moment, Britt shakes her head as if to say that nothing's wrong. Of course, there are the tears, the tissues, and the tortured look on her face.

"It's just—"

"What, sweetie?"

"He's gone. I know it. I woke up and I felt it. Just like that. I know in my heart that James is gone."

"Did you hear anything—"

"No. We're never going to hear anything. That's why I know. That's why I'm feeling this way."

Beth is able to exhale as she slips onto the bed beside Britt. "Why do you suddenly feel this way?"

"Everything is wrong."

"Talk to me. What happened since this afternoon?"

"I had a lousy night with Richie. He was so unbelievably fussy. And for once I just wanted to let my

husband take care of him. Is that too much to ask? Is
that too much to ask God?"

"No."

Britt blows her nose and then tosses the tissue onto
the pile on her bed.

"I shouldn't have watched that stupid movie. That's
what did it."

"What did you watch?"

"It's my own fault. Mine and Tom Hanks's."

Beth imagines *Saving Private Ryan* or *Band of
Brothers*. Maybe the recent series on HBO called *The
Pacific*.

"Which movie? What was it?"

"*Sleepless in Seattle*."

After what Beth was thinking, the title almost makes
her chuckle. That's about the last movie Beth would
picture. Then again, it makes perfect sense.

"I'm sorry, sweetie."

"I've seen that movie a dozen times. But tonight,
I don't know. Something about it. Something about
watching it alone. James hated that movie but deep
down he's a romantic. That's why he likes writing. He's
able to write things he normally can't say. It's not in a
soldier's nature to be flowery and poetic and gushing.
Yet that's who James is."

"You're right," Beth says.

"Do you know that when he deployed to Afghanistan,

he'd already left a few days before actually leaving? He stripped himself of his emotion and put on that armor that made him tough. He barely said good-bye."

"It was his way."

"I know. And that way—his way, the army way—was supposed to keep him alive. You know? So what? So what happened then?"

"We don't know."

"But I feel like I know. I really do."

"You watched a movie tonight. That's all. You miss him the way we all do."

"I never thought it'd be like this."

Beth rubs her hands and notices how dry they are. She glances at them and they don't even look like her own. They resemble the frail hands of some middle-aged woman who's spent too much time rubbing them, too much time keeping them busy, too much time adding wrinkles to their edges.

"Life doesn't work out like those movies," she says. "Or more like—the movies don't show it all. They show the sparks, the romance, the pretty pictures. The nice, neat drama that leads to the happy ending. But life isn't always that way. Your story, Britt—your story with James—is a beautiful one. How you stuck together. Your wedding day. How you found out you were pregnant. It's a beautiful story."

"I just want to know the ending."

"None of us knows the ending."

"The ending to *this* story. That's all I ask. So I'll be able to live and maybe create other ones."

"I know." Beth sighs. "Sometimes I think I'm the exact opposite, that I don't want to know the ending. I'm afraid to find out because I won't like the outcome."

"But you want to know."

"I just want James back. Like you. I don't want that story to be over. Just the chapter."

James

April 14, 2007

Dear Mom:

I know I've been writing to you for some time, but this really feels like my first official letter. Maybe that's because I'm writing this from Camp Liberty. I'm no longer training. No longer in airborne school. I'm no longer wondering when the time will come. I'm here and it's real.

It's funny, too, because for some reason, I've been picturing this vast hot desert in Iraq. But it's still pretty cold over here. I think it's colder than it is in Johnson City at this time of the year. You gotta love the ironies of perceptions.

The guys in my unit are good ones. I've got a couple of Vols fans out here, believe it or not. A few of them are married, even have kids. Maybe I was expecting a bunch of Rambos, but it's not been like that at all. Hollywood's portrayal of soldiers, especially in this war, doesn't always turn out to be accurate.

Dad used to say that all the time. Though it didn't stop him from watching all those John Wayne movies, huh?

This place reminds me of Dad. I think of the stories he used to tell me about coming over here. Sometimes I think I made them up. I don't know. But I've been thinking about him. About you guys.

I'm glad Dad told me what it was like to be a soldier in the army.

Then that makes me think of Britt. And of the day I'll meet my son—and get to be a father myself.

I'd love that. Not necessarily to have a son to go in the military, but to have a child who would look up to me and love me. To be able to mold and shape that child.

Such a thought.

I miss you guys but remain excited to be here. Will hopefully be able to talk with you soon! Hug Britt for me.

Love,
James

April 22, 2007

Dear James,

I love talking to you, but I still adore getting your letters. They're special and I know that you get that. I can reread them. I guess I could record our conversations too but that's just not the same as reading your thoughts and feelings.

I'm so glad that things are going well for you. I look forward to hearing about your day-to-day duties. I'm curious. As your mother, I hope they're monotonous instead of harrowing. Action and suspense are fine if they're in a Tom Clancy novel, but I don't want them in one of your letters. Please.

Emily and I have been butting heads lately. Maybe it's normal. She's got all sorts of ideas of where she "wants" to go to college. Universities in Florida and California seem to really be attracting her attention. She's so smart but she's so headstrong. It seems as if she just wants to get far away from me.

I can just hear you now. And yes, I know. I don't want both of my children living miles away.

If that is part of the plan, I can accept it. But with Emily, I don't think she understands what "plan" means. You always had a plan. You always knew. Emily seems to discover what she knows with each passing day.

Britt has been coming over on a regular basis. I don't mean to complain about Emily—she's been so wonderful and so open with Britt. She's already accepted her as a sister. It's hard to be frustrated with Em when she turns around and does stuff like that.

Summer doesn't seem far away and the regular schedule is going to be kicking in. We're going to miss having you around, especially when everybody gets together on Memorial Day. The parade and the party just won't be the same without you.

I love you and I'm praying all the time for you. Be careful and safe and make sure you stay in touch. At least one of my children can fill me in on what he's thinking and feeling—even if he's all the way over in another world.

Hope to hear from you soon.

Mom

May 2, 2007

Dear Mom:

I experienced my first bomb.

How's that for an opening line? Well I did, but I only just heard it. It might have been miles away.

There's nothing to report, good or bad. I am thankful. But there's this funny thing I've been thinking about while here.

All this training and readiness. I know I'm physically fit and mentally strong, but deep down inside—that's what I wonder about, Mom.

I can't tell any of these guys. There are guys who look terrified yet they're the ones who act the most macho. You can just see the fear in their eyes. I don't pretend I'm tough. Yet I still doubt.

If the time comes when I know without question that I'm going to have to take a life, will I be brave? Will I flinch?

It's one thing to stand guard and to patrol and to beware of all the possible signs.

But in battle, in the heat of the moment, will I be ready?

I pray I will but I don't know.

Some of the stories—soldiers getting killed for being stupid, for not being attentive, for simply walking the wrong path—make you think.

Keep praying, Mom. The security of your prayers is more reassuring than the rifle in my arms.

I should be talking to you any day now. Look forward to hearing your voice.

Love you,
James

May 13, 2007

Dear James,

It was so amazing to talk to you. Also a bit surreal. It felt like you were at home with Britt, that you guys were going to come over to Sunday dinner, that we were all going to be together for a while. Thanks so much for calling and surprising me.

I've been seeing a lot of Britt, trying to keep her spirits high. She puts on a good front, but I know it's hard for her. All I can do is share that I've been in her shoes. I know how difficult waiting and wondering can be. Even when you're able to call or e-mail or write—or yes, even Skype (though don't push that on me!!).

I'm including a picture that I took of Britt the other day. She's so beautiful.

I know it's got to be difficult—even on the boring days. I pray your days continue to be calm and quiet. Keep on being a positive role model for the other soldiers you're with. You might not believe it but I know you are one. Stay strong.

Surprise me any time you like with a call! I welcome it. Along with your continued letters.

Love you,
Mom

Beth

"I'm thinking of going to Chicago this summer."

Emily's comment makes about as much sense as a green alien knocking on the door and asking for a place to spend the night.

"What?"

Sometimes a single word can be so much more. A single word combined with a skeptical laugh and a bewildered scowl along with a dismissive posture and tone . . . well, sometimes a "What?" can mean much, much more.

"There's an outdoor music festival that's taking place in early August."

If Beth hadn't already asked "What?" she'd do it again.

She closes the dishwasher that she'd asked Emily earlier to unload, then walks into the family room where her daughter is standing.

"What music festival?"

"It's called Lollapalooza."

"Lolla-what?"

"It's where a bunch of bands go and play in a park in the middle of Chicago."

"Chicago? So what—you're just going to drive there?"

"Trish is driving. A bunch of people are going."

"Oh, okay."

"What?"

"Nothing," Beth says.

"Are you saying I can't go?"

"Are you asking me permission?"

"No," Emily says, but she sounds uncertain.

"How long will you be gone?"

"The fest is Friday to Sunday. So we'd probably go Thursday and come back on a Monday."

"What about your job?"

"They're fine."

"You already asked them?"

"Sure. They don't care. They have enough servers wanting to work."

"And you're not one of them?"

"I'm going to take some time off before going back to school."

"So you're taking the whole month of August off?"

Emily is looking at her iPhone.

She's always looking at that thing and never looking at me.

"Emily—"

"What?"

"Do you want to go out of spite?"

Her daughter's gaze meets her own. There's a fire in that look, a kind that sometimes scares her.

It's like looking at Richard.

"Out of spite?" Emily asks. "For what?"

"I don't know. Just—things."

"They've got some great groups playing this year. I had to miss last year."

"I was hoping we could do a few things before the end of the summer."

"You said that at the beginning of summer."

"I know."

And thanks for reminding me, too.

"I've been around, Mom."

"I've been busy."

"Busy? Busy at what?"

"Can you put that phone down and look at me?"

Emily does so and the feisty look intensifies.

"You know all the things I do."

"Yeah, like babysit Britt."

"Em, don't say that."

"It's true. And it's fine. But I don't need babysitting, Mom. I've already told you that."

"I'm not talking about babysitting."

"Then what *are* you talking about? Taking a trip to James's military base? Or how about going by to see Dad's gravestone? Or maybe renting *Schindler's List*?"

"Stop it."

"I don't want to look back, Mom. I'm tired of looking back. I'm tired of waiting to hear something. Don't you get sick of it?"

She wants to reply. She only nods.

"I've been here almost a month, Mom. You're so busy and yet—what? When are you going to decide there's time for me?"

"This trip—are you going because you're angry?" she asks again.

Emily laughs. "I'm going because I like a bunch of the bands playing. That's all. That and the fact that it's summer. And I'm twenty-one. *I'm* not in the army, Mom."

"Don't."

"Then you don't," Emily says. "It's a weekend. A long weekend. It's a fun break. And it's not for another month."

"Maybe I could go with."

"Oh, yeah, you'd love that. The heat and the crowds and the loud music."

"Maybe I *should* go."

"You'd have to check with the army first, right? You

have to tell them where you're going to be at all times. Can't go off the 'base.'"

"What's gotten into you today?"

"I don't know. Nothing."

"Em, what is it?"

"I already told you. It's just that being here—it reminds me of all the things that you've gone through."

"That we've gone through."

"I'd rather not have to remember. It's easier that way."

———

Beth?

"Yes. Here I am."

She's here but she's still unwilling.

It's nighttime and the melancholy shadows have surfaced. They're coming too frequently these days. They're not going away as often as they normally would.

Beth recalls the familiar story but sees it in a whole new light.

She wonders if she could do the same.

Take your son, your only son . . .

He's already gone, she thinks in the silence of the house. *He's already sacrificed.*

Beth?

The voice in her head says her name over and over again. It's just her mind playing tricks, the silence getting to her, the demons of doubt whispering words in her ear.

Then again, she thinks, *maybe it's not demons. Maybe it's God trying to get to me, trying to test me.*

Or maybe free you.

It's nighttime and she's just about ready to write James a letter.

Where is the lamb for the sacrifice?

All this time. All these months. Almost two whole years.

Has all of this—the letters and the praying and the worry and the believing—has all of it been for nothing? Has it been wrong for her to carry all of this?

Beth thinks of her daughter's words. Then she recalls the angel's words to Abraham.

I know that you truly fear God. You have not withheld even your beloved son from me.

Holding the pen in her hand, Beth wonders. Is she still holding back? Has she truly given everything to God?

There is hope in this world. But there is also letting go.

"Lord, please show me the difference. Show me how to fear you and how to withhold *nothing*."

She knows that even though she prays, she's not ready. Not yet.

She needs help letting go. But there's no one around who can truly guide her through that.

But maybe there's something that will help. Something that you need to do. Something that you've put off for so many years. Maybe it's time.

Beth buries the thought.

———

So maybe there are a few good reasons for Beth to have a Facebook page. Emily's just shown her one.

For quite some time, Beth has been against getting one. The first reason is she doesn't want the invasion of privacy. The second is that—well, that pertains to privacy too. Most of the reasons have to do with keeping her life her own.

She doesn't want a page for people to send their prayers and commentary. There are already several pages up for James and that's fine. She can respect people wanting to remember and lift James up in prayer. But she does not need a thousand comments a day saying how and why and when they're praying for her or telling her how to handle his absence. Especially when they're strangers who don't know James or her.

Yet just a moment ago, Emily informed Beth that she received a message from her friend Josie. She was one of those people who spent lots of time uploading photos from family trips and fun onto her Facebook page. She also tweeted or whatever it was called.

Emily reads the message and says, "Josie says since

you don't have a page yourself, she wanted to send it to me. It says, 'Have your mom check this out. It would be fun to go to!'"

"How can you read on that thing?"

"It's not that small, Mom."

"I don't think I want to know what she wants me to check out. Please tell me it doesn't involve men who look like Tom Selleck."

"Tom who?"

"Sometimes you make me feel really old, you know that?"

Emily smiles. "Well, I don't want to tell you—"

"No. Stop. Don't continue that thought."

"It's nothing to do with men. It's some kind of horse stable."

Emily shows her on her phone but she can't make out anything.

"I need my glasses," Beth says.

Emily shrugs and then mouths the word "old."

"It's got a bunch of horses you can ride. Sounds like Josie wants to take you horseback riding."

"She's been on me about doing lots of things."

"Why don't you?"

"Speed dating isn't my thing."

"Yeah, but you planning on dating a horse?"

"There are probably a lot more horses out there that I'd like to spend time with than men."

Emily laughs. "Does Josie ride a lot?"

"Josie does everything a lot."

There's a certain tone in her response that almost echoes off the walls around her.

"Just sayin'," Emily adds.

"Well maybe your mother is going to start doing lots more things too. Just sayin'."

"Like getting a Facebook page?"

"Let's not go overboard."

James

July 19, 2007

Dear Mom:

War is hell, Mom. It really is.

It is the culmination of hate and violence and want and greed. The face of bigotry and prejudice. The hand of the devil that only destroys.

The devil recently paid our unit a visit.

There was a guy named Rodriguez who was supposed to return home in less than thirty days.

He wasn't blown up with some suicide bomb or cut down by enemy fire. He was killed brandishing his weapon and charging the enemy—he was killed during a simple training exercise.

Of course nothing is simple, especially out here. Things happen. Right?

I'm struggling with this.

He had a wife and two kids back home. He was going to leave the army when his commitments were done. Finish up school. Be a father and get on with life.

I wish God would let me know why.

It's hard enough seeing the blood of a fallen brother, but to see a life lost like this. Such a waste.

Pray for his family, Mom. Pray for his wife and children.

I can still hear his laugh sometimes in my dreams. I'll wake up wondering if he's around the corner.

I really want to come home.

James

July 27, 2007

Dear James,

We're praying for you during this difficult time.

Three Bible verses come to mind that give me hope.

Psalm 34:18—"The Lord is close to the brokenhearted and saves those who are crushed in spirit."

John 14:27—"Peace I leave with you; my peace I give you. I do not give to you as the world gives. Do not let your hearts be troubled and do not be afraid."

And 1 John 5:14–15—"This is the confidence we have in approaching God: that if we ask anything according to his will, he hears us. And if we know that he hears us— whatever we ask—we know that we have what we asked of him."

I will be praying for you and for your unit as well as Rodriguez's family.

Keep these verses and other passages close at hand and close to your heart. Bring them out even when you don't feel like reading them. Remind yourself of them and others when you are low and angry and confused.

Please call when you can.

Love,
Mom

August 4, 2007

Dear Mom:

I apologize for getting all introspective and melancholy in these letters. Whenever I write the words "Dear Mom," I think I start to get a bit sad. I miss you and Emily and Britt and everybody else.

I'll try to lighten the mood. At least this time.

I shared what happened to Rodriguez. But let me tell you about some of the other guys in my unit. They are something else.

There's Mac. That's his nickname. He's a crazy Irish guy who's a bit obsessed with Britt and thinks she should marry him (the redheaded connection, I guess). He's from Baltimore and likes playing video games.

There's Bruce, and he's one of those conspiracy guys. Thinks that Elvis is still alive, that the government killed JFK, that the war in Iraq is part of a bigger conspiracy. He's an X-Files nut and loves that show. Lost too. He's always talking in a hushed tone about some kind of cover-up.

Bruce is tight with Jackson, who writes fiction. He dreams of writing military thrillers. I see him writing a lot. He asks me about these letters and then wonders if I've ever tried writing. He's always reading something, too, and is constantly telling me books and authors I need to check out.

There's Sam, who looks like he's on steroids. Maybe he is. He's always working out. He moves like a tank.

There's Carter, who's from Alabama and has the thickest accent in the world. Sometimes even I can't understand him.

So many guys—these are just snapshots. I can't really do justice to them, or to the stuff we've seen and the stuff that's happened to us.

I don't want you to worry. I'm with some great guys. Really.

Sometimes this war and this place get to me but not most of the time. Most of the time I'm doing okay.

Most of the time I'm doing just fine.

Love you!
James

Beth

The big white set of teeth seems to surround her the way a picket fence might surround a graveyard. A never-ending smile from a never-ending siphon.

I can't do it. I don't want to do it. Not again. Not this year.

Beth's bones feel attached like tectonic plates, rubbing against one another, just bracing for the eventual earthquake. Nobody can see this on the surface, but she feels the chafing every day.

She wants to hurl the cup of expensive coffee at the wannabe politician in front of her and run for the glass door and then keep running.

What's gotten into me lately? What's my problem?

"We're counting on you," Sonny Stephenson says, that grin going like the Energizer bunny.

She has the craziest thought, thinking of Sonny's initials and then thinking they actually fit him.

"I don't think I can do it this year."

"Oh, come on, Beth, you gotta be in it. No walking necessary. I promise. You can ride on our float."

Of course I can.

"We just want to remember James and what he stood for."

Of course you do.

The southern drawl and smile really don't help Sonny's cause. Beth knows that the businessman is just doing his job, and that maybe deep down he really does care for what James *stands* for.

"I'm just not sure I'm up for being in the parade," Beth says. "This year."

Sonny sees someone else who calls out his name, and this is how Beth breaks it off. She is having coffee, or trying to have coffee, with Leah. Her friend is at a booth in the corner, a place where Beth can sit with her back to all the potential Sonnys who might want to come up to her and talk.

When did I become so antisocial, so uncivil?

She tells Leah about the awkward interaction. Leah can't help but laugh, knowing Sonny and why he wants her in the parade.

"You know you're a celebrity, even though for an awful reason," Leah says to her.

Leah can say that because Leah understands. She's a mother of two boys in the service, both stationed in Afghanistan. Leah has taken it upon herself to buy coffee for Beth as often as she'll indulge, which is about every other week. This little act is a big blessing.

"He got to me already, though you know me," Leah says, "I'm always doing it. I'm a sucker for anything related to celebrating the military and waving a flag. Especially on the Fourth."

"I used to be too."

Leah's grip is as strong as her heart. "And you will continue to be. You can be proud to be a wife and a mother of a soldier. That never has to change."

"Sometimes I want a break."

"And sometimes you *need* a break, and loudmouths like Sonny can deal with it. But just know why you're taking a break, that's all I ask."

Beth sighs. "I don't know. Things have suddenly gotten a lot worse."

"With what?"

"With everything. The waiting. The silence. The not knowing."

"How's Emily?"

"She's not exactly supportive. Maybe that's one reason why—why it's suddenly become this giant issue I can't get around day after day."

Leah opens her mouth and her face contorts to an expression of exaggerated surprise. Richard once told

Beth that all southern women have this look and this expression, one of mild shock.

"How can she not be?"

"Because it's been so long," Beth says. "She wants to move on. And I don't blame her."

"You won't be able to move on until you know what happens."

"And I've told her that. But still—it's the way she's coping."

Sonny comes back over to their table to say good-bye and to pat Beth on the back. "You let me know if you can make it. It'd sure mean a lot if you could. Y'all ladies have a great day now."

Leah smiles and then rolls her eyes when Sonny is leaving the shop.

"I can't," Beth says. "I just can't."

"I know and I get it. But understand something, okay? When you walk or ride in the parade, you don't walk as a soccer mom or a politician or a woman telling everybody about her new coffee shop. You walk as one of us. You walk as James. You walk to have people remember—to have people realize the real meaning of this holiday."

The coffee is still warm against her hands, but the rest of her is cold.

"People grow so accustomed to not knowing anything and frankly, to not caring. But, Beth, when you walk, people who do know will remember. And they'll tell others. They'll say, 'That's the mother of James Thompson, the MIA.'"

"I know. I just don't know if I'm up for being a poster child this year."

"Sometimes in life—many times, I think—God wants us to be someone or something that we don't want. But you know, it's not up to us. We don't control anything. We have to be the people He wants us to be. That might be a heavy responsibility, but He's not going to give it to someone who ultimately can't handle it."

"I can't handle this."

"You can handle anything that comes your way and I know it," Leah says. "I might weigh twice as much as you do, but you're a lot stronger than me."

"Stop being silly."

"I might be silly but I *always* speak the truth. Always."

———

Beth hangs up the phone but feels like doing more. She feels like digging a hole in the backyard and tossing the cordless inside it. Along with the television and the radio and the computer and any connection to the outside world.

"Who was that?" Emily asks.

"Another reporter."

"Sorry. I shouldn't have picked it up."

"It's okay. By now I know what to say."

"So why are you so upset?"

"Most of the times the reporters know what to say back. But this woman didn't want to take a no. As if she was calling for Oprah herself."

"Was she?"

"No." Beth laughs. "And I'd say the same to her, too, if she still had her show."

Over the past two years, Beth has learned about the media and its bloodthirsty machinery. Everybody wants a good story, and everybody wanted *her* story. After granting a few interviews with the local news, Beth decided to stop doing anything more. But the fact that Sergeant First Class James Thompson was one of the only two MIAs so far in the Afghanistan war didn't make things easy.

Don't forget about Sabi. Don't dare forget about her.

Sabi had been MIA for fourteen months.

She served with a joint Australian-Afghan army patrol that was ambushed in September 2008. After the battle, during which nine troops were wounded, there was no sign of Sabi, and the subsequent months of searching didn't result in anything.

It wasn't until November of 2009 that she was found. Where she had been, nobody knows.

And they never will, either, since Sabi's a black Labrador.

Every now and then, Beth liked to think of Sabi. She sometimes invented stories involving Sabi and James. Of course, James went missing in 2009, but logic didn't factor into those fantasies.

If a dog can go missing for fourteen months in the wilds of Afghanistan, my son, an Eighty-second Airborne Division paratrooper, can still be alive after two years.

"What's wrong?" Emily asks.

She can't tell Emily since the name "Sabi" has been banned from the Thompson house by Emily. It became an anecdote of the war that soon grew into a grim punch line as the months became years.

"Just wondering when it will stop. If it ever will."

"The calls?"

"All of it."

"Maybe you do one big interview and that's it. That's not waving the white flag, Mom. You can say so in the interview."

"I don't know. I don't want to open the floodgates."

"Maybe we should disconnect the phone."

"I've already thought about doing that. But they've caught me on the street, on my lawn, even at church."

"Who?"

"Nobody worth mentioning."

"It's like you're someone famous being hounded by the paparazzi."

"It just gets worse around this time of year. People

want a moving story to show on television to the families gathering for their July Fourth parties."

Emily wears a familiar look of sadness and confusion on her pretty face.

"I don't blame them for wanting that story, either. I just keep . . ."

She doesn't finish.

Emily doesn't need her to finish, either.

They've heard it over and over and over again.

I just keep hoping to know the outcome.

But maybe there will never be one.

Maybe this story will have to be told when she finally takes her last breath and walks through the pearly gates of heaven.

———

"You sound like I normally do."

Beth chuckles. "Maybe you're being a bad influence."

"And maybe you're just being a mother. Have you ever thought of that?"

"Something about this summer—about having Emily back home and her attitude—about the coming anniversary. I don't know."

"It's okay," Marion tells her.

"Is it? I don't know. This isn't like me."

"If you didn't grieve you wouldn't be human."

"But sometimes I just—I feel like I'm being tested."

"I've been tested every single day of my life since becoming a mother. Raising that Francisco was enough to kill me, and that's *before* he went missing. Sons don't understand what they do to their mothers."

"Neither do daughters."

"If you're being tested, so be it."

"What do you mean?" Beth asks.

"Ace it. That's what I used to tell the kids. Ace the exams. Not just those in the class but those in life. Take the test and do your best and make sure you come out with your head held high."

"You're rhyming."

"Am I?" Marion asks. "Maybe I should be a poet."

"Are you reading me something from a motivational handbook?"

"Now you're really sounding a lot like me."

"Or my daughter." Beth lets out a sigh. "They're wanting me to be in the July Fourth parade again."

"And you will, of course."

"Of course."

"That is part of the drill. Or maybe I should say part of the test. You can't decide not to take it anymore. That will be with you the rest of your life."

"What?"

"Your role. Our role. We are mothers to soldiers who have given their lives for their country. It's just—the country is holding its breath along with us to see whether or not those lives are still there or not."

"I wish everybody would just continue breathing."

"That's what I see you doing. That's what you've been doing for almost two years now."

"I'm turning over a new leaf," Beth says. "And it's wet and rotten on the other side."

"No you don't, young lady."

"You're just a couple years older than I am."

"Don't get that way. I'm the one who freaks out and you're the one who stays grounded. We can't shift roles."

"Not even every now and then?"

"No way. I need to have my July Fourth freak-out and I need to know that my Elizabeth Thompson will be there to anchor me."

"I will always be here, Marion. Even on days like this."

"There will be a time, you know."

"I know."

"There will be a time when we find out. And I just—*I'm* going to need you."

"We're going to need each other."

"Ace it. Go out and show every single person at that parade how dignified and proud you are. Show them and ace it."

July 3, 2011

Dear James,

I'm not going to lie—today has been difficult. This week has been difficult. I'm praying about tomorrow because I know it will be difficult.

I know God doesn't promise us that every day will be full of joy and hope. I know that He asks us not to be afraid. But there are times when I feel like it's all too much.

When I wish I could have gone missing.

It's a selfish and foolish thing to say, James. I know that. But I'm sitting here writing to myself, talking to myself, telling myself stories. My psyche doesn't even benefit from these letters.

They're doing nobody any good.

These are days when I get tired of the war, tired of the hate out there, tired of the ignorance of friends and family.

There are days when my body and my mind and my soul are just plain tired.

I need rest.

They talk about the living waters of God but sometimes I think I need to die to see them.

These are the times when it's the most difficult to pray and to write. It's been so long. And yet.

And yet.

Nearly two years have been summed up with two words: "and yet."

Maybe one day I'll know and I'll understand.

Tonight, however, I'll just pray to make it to tomorrow. I'll pray for sleep to come and for me to swim in those living waters, even if they're a mirage.

I'll pray for you once again, knowing that God hears the prayers, even those uttered a thousand times. Maybe He will answer them. Maybe He will at least take a slight burden off my shoulders.

I hope that if you're out there, wherever you might be, God does the same.

Your loving
mother

—

The colors bleed over her. Beth sees the crowd in slow motion, the tiny hands waving little flags, the lawn chairs resting on the grass, the T-shirts and smiles passing her by. There is so much red, white, and blue, yet all she can think is that there should be only one color today.

Everyone should wear red to mark all those killed in every war since the beginning of time.

Her grin and her wave are permanent fixtures on this float. She can get through this. People know who she is and why she's here, and she's smiling and waving to show support. But to these people this holiday is just that: a day off, a chance to eat and mingle, an excuse to lounge around, a leisurely day topped off by colorful fireworks.

Some men and women see fireworks year round. They get to hear louder explosions—some actually get to be in those very explosions.

Beth remembers holding James on her lap and sitting in one of those lawn chairs. He would wave his flag and rush into the street after it got littered with candy by one of the clowns. She would cover his ears when the fire trucks blasted their sirens. She would wipe his mouth once he got finished with his purple sucker. She would carry him back after he fell asleep in her arms.

She wants him to fall asleep in her arms, just one more

time. She wants to feel that big body of his crushing her own. He could scoop her up with one arm, that is how strong he is now. But it doesn't matter, because he will forever be her little boy, just like the freckled faces that glance at her as she passes and waves.

The music and the grins and the saluting and the flags and the red, white, and blue feel like a vise against her head and her heart. Tightening, squeezing, pounding, beating away.

This is supposed to be a holiday but for her it is becoming a cross to bear. She knows what she is supposed to do with that, where she is supposed to go with that.

So tell me, God, how much longer is this parade going to last? How much farther do I have to go in this float?

Beth is good at staying strong. But on this muggy July Fourth, she suddenly realizes that appearing good at something doesn't necessarily mean you are.

I don't know how much longer I can be strong. The ground beneath is giving way and shaking and I'm starting to crumble and fall over.

"Hi, Beth!" a voice calls out.

She sees Leah and waves and smiles back.

She's feeling this way because this is what her life the last two years has been like: surrounded and applauded and cheered, but from a distance. Seen by spectators who try but don't truly understand. Those who understand are marching with her. They are carrying the flags and driving the cars and marching in the parade.

I need to get out of this parade and back on the curb. I need to start living again even if it's without that little boy sitting on my lap.

Because somewhere, there's a little girl who's gotten lost in the parade.

—

The smile is as refreshing as a cup of lemonade on a scorching summer day.

"You look as pretty as you did when you were on the homecoming court."

"Shush," Beth jokes with Joel. "I don't want anybody knowing we're the same age."

"They wouldn't believe me if I tried. This bald head has always made me look ten years older."

"That earns you respect, though. You need it when you're coaching."

"Anything to get high school boys' attention is welcome. How're you doing today?"

"Fine. Thanks."

"You're still such an actress. Even after all these years."

"And you're still a flirt. That's why Richard never liked you."

"Smart man, that Richard. He was wise."

Joel Stirling barks out to one of his four kids as he

stands next to Beth. They both graduated from Science Hill High School, where Joel has coached varsity football for the last ten years.

"Man, I miss James," Joel says.

"Thanks."

"No, I mean really miss him. Our team could use a fullback like him. They don't make kids like that anymore. That tough."

"We bought him that way," Beth jokes. "A little more expensive but worth it."

"I'm serious. I tell my boys about James, about how he used to catch a ball and go looking for someone to ram into. Some kids try to sneak off the sidelines. James wanted to hit somebody. All the time."

"That's my boy."

Joel looks at her and smiles. "That strength isn't something you inherit from just one parent, you know."

"So I've been told."

"Hanging in there?"

"Well—I am wanting to tackle a few people. Would sure feel good."

"We could arrange that," Joel says with a chuckle.

As his family begins to head toward the parked car, Joel invites Beth over to their house for lunch.

"Thanks. That's very kind of you."

"I'm not just asking because I'm the only other

widower. I just thought you might like the company. Emily and you."

"I have to go find her. She's disappeared."

Joel looks toward his children. "Looks like mine are about to do the same."

Beth knows that he's a good father, especially after having to take care of the family when his wife passed away several years ago.

"You better go," she says.

"Offer is open all day. For fireworks, too."

"Thanks."

"And hey—if you need someone to tackle, well, I *am* a football coach."

"You also never change."

———

"Emily?"

The only sound that greets her is a breeze coming through the kitchen window.

She walks upstairs and finds Emily's room empty.

It shouldn't surprise her, yet it does.

There is a note on her dresser. *Mom—heading to see the fireworks with some friends. Don't wait up. Emily.*

She puts the note back on the dresser and then sits at the edge of her bed. She's not surprised.

She knows what this means.

It will be the first time she can remember that Emily won't be with her for the fireworks celebration. They always went as a family, even when it was just the three of them. They continued the tradition when it was just the two of them.

Now I'm by myself.

Yet she has only herself to blame.

Before the parade there had been an argument. Beth had been so stressed that she hadn't really paid Emily much attention. Emily said to call her later and Beth forgot.

I deserve to be on my own.

She thinks of calling Emily now but then stops herself. Her daughter is old enough to be with friends and make her own decisions. She's not a baby anymore.

And Mom doesn't need babysitting either.

Beth closes her eyes. Her face is sore from smiling so much. She doesn't know how celebrities and politicians do it all the time.

She stands back up and heads downstairs. She puts some dirty cups and bowls in the dishwasher, then takes some leftovers out of the refrigerator and throws them away. She opens a bottle of water and takes it out to her backyard.

It's the time of day on a summer evening when the oranges and the reds seem to be blooming in the sky. She smells the scent of a barbecue and can hear the sounds of neighborhood kids laughing and calling out in the background. The tree limbs jostle gently like the wave of a queen.

Her glance goes above the trees to the sky.

Can you see me, Richard?

She normally doesn't do this because it feels so pointless to wonder and worry. But all the suppressed feelings of the day—all the smiles and thank-yous and the small talk and the appreciation she didn't really ask for—are now starting to seep out of her pores.

She sips her bottle of water and feels like having a glass of wine instead.

Am I doing something wrong? What should I be doing? More? Less?

Silence is a hard thing to get used to. There were times when both of the kids would be crying, or later, as they got older, fighting. Those were times when the sweet sound of silence felt like an illusion, something sacred and impossible to find. She and Richard sometimes felt as if they were in a marathon that was never over.

Richard and I.

He was always there. They were a team. And that's what is different now. The band is broken up and she is going solo. It wasn't in any of their plans except God's. There has to be a reason why but she doesn't know and won't know until she gets to heaven.

People always do better when they're working in a team. That's the beauty of marriage.

A loud explosion goes off in the distance. She can't help but think of James.

So many things are reminders. The obvious and the not so obvious.

"Lord, help me find the words with Emily. Help me to know what to do and what to say."

As she glances at a patch of clouds in the distance, she wonders if her daughter is doing the same.

———

The cracks and pops of fireworks continue to go off even though it's around eleven. Emily hasn't come home, and Beth knows that it's probably best to talk in the morning. As she gets ready for bed, going through her regular routine, she stops as she holds the cream-colored stationery in her hand.

No.

She puts it away and turns off the light.

Enough.

Nothing is going to happen to him if she doesn't write a letter. Nothing is going to change if she doesn't put a stamp on it and mail it out. Nothing is going to be any different—nothing whatsoever—if she decides to simply go to bed.

She still prays but she finds herself having a hard time doing it.

This house feels so big. This bed so big. Everything so big and myself so small.

Why have I been writing for so long? All these wasted words for what? Written for whom? I might as well have written to Santa Claus.

She tries to sleep but she can't.

The thoughts continue to rage inside her, mocking her, telling her she's a fool to believe.

A blast outside reminds her of the date.

This is a time for families to be together. To celebrate. Holidays are for families.

She feels her body shake.

She does not know why God has left her alone like this.

Emily is grown and soon the summer will be over and she'll be heading back to school.

Richard will continue to be a memory. A shadow of a man she loved and married. Footprints in the sand on the beach of their honeymoon. Tracks in the snow on the grounds of the first army base they lived at.

Soon, James will be the same. A memory. A name and an image and ten thousand memories. But that's all.

I'm not strong enough.

She feels a tear edge out and fall down onto her pillow.

Why today and why now she doesn't know. It's happened before and will surely happen again.

She knows she needs to talk to others. To family and friends. To the "family readiness group" that she's done a great job of avoiding. She can't keep everything inside and can't keep up this image of strength.

The sound of the door opening gives her a small measure of peace.

Not tonight and not now.

She needs to talk to Emily but needs to find the right time and the right words. If such things exist.

Beth knows that all of them—Richard, James, Emily, herself—have found themselves at crucial points in their lives. Beth is at one of them the same way her daughter is.

She thinks back and remembers when James came home after his time in Iraq. He was just as they are, someone needing to find his place in life.

Eventually, sooner or later, we all come to that fork in the road of life. We all get there and have to look in the mirror in order to figure out which way to go.

James

When James awoke, he wasn't sure where he was.

For a second, he thought he was still in Iraq. He was having a beer with Rodriguez, laughing about something, making fun of the guy. Good times.

His eyes took a while to focus and he saw a cuckoo clock. He realized he was in the family room of their house.

His last memory was of drinking beers with the guys outside at the keg party.

Uh-oh.

He tried to open his mouth and felt throbbing. His palm grazed his cheek and felt the mound, as if his mouth was full of tobacco.

This wasn't good.

He wasn't in Iraq and wasn't wearing his camo and wasn't remembering the last dozen hours of his life.

James sat up and felt the ocean swell against one side of this boat, then crash and roll over against the other side.

The problem was he wasn't in a boat but in his mom's house.

For a few minutes, he managed to try to focus. To remember. To start running all systems again.

But the memory chip was not working.

Standing up made things worse for a moment. He eventually walked into the kitchen. A coffee mug was resting next to the full pot of coffee.

On another counter was a bottle of water next to a bottle of aspirin.

He took the aspirin and water first, knowing they'd help a little. The only thing that was really going to help him was time. Time to flush the toxins out of his system. Time to survey the damage. Time to apologize to everyone he needed to apologize to.

He drained the bottle of water, then poured some coffee. Then he heard the shuffling coming from the hallway.

"Morning," he said to his mother.

"I'd say good morning, but we already passed it," Mom said with a look that resembled the one she wore at his father's funeral. "Plus, there's nothing good about this morning."

This wasn't going to be pretty.

———

"How did this happen?"

James had already finished a cup of coffee and was managing to get some semblance of gravity and motor skills working again.

"I think it involved a little too much alcohol."

The joke didn't go over very well. He had already apologized to his mother several times.

"I don't know," he said. "The night must've gotten out of hand."

"You don't even remember what happened?"

"No."

"There was a fight. You're lucky you weren't arrested. Instead they called me. I told Harvey he should've just thrown you in jail. But he didn't want to do that. Especially since you didn't instigate it. And since your buddies pretty much ended whatever was started."

"Who? Carter? Lance?"

"I don't know and I don't care. I just want to know how this happened."

"Mom, I already told you—"

"What have you been doing over there?"

"Over where?"

"Where do you think?" she said. "In Iraq."

He shook his head and then rubbed his temple. The throbbing hadn't gone away. Her loud voice wasn't helping.

"Mom, I'm not a little boy anymore."

"Are you getting into bad habits?"

"No."

"Then what do you call this?"

"This isn't something I do on a daily basis, okay?"

"What's going on then?"

James could try to tell her but he didn't have the words to explain. He didn't have the words or the energy. It would be easier simply writing her a letter when the fog in his head cleared.

"Nothing," he said.

"Don't give me that. As long as you're in this house, you need to explain things like this."

"I won't be here for much longer."

"You think Britt is going to put up with this? I haven't told her yet."

"Like she hasn't seen me this way."

"You two are getting married in three months. She's not going to want to marry and live with someone like that."

"Someone like what?" James snapped back.

"The someone who got drunk last night."

"You just—you don't get it."

His mom stood at the table he was sitting at and slammed her hands against the top of a chair. "What don't I get? You think this is the first time I've seen someone come home from a war?"

"Mom, come on."

"No, don't give me that. You think I don't understand? I was married to your father. I know. I *understand*, James, so do not give me that."

"Yeah, well, this isn't a habit."

"But it might become one."

"No, Mom. I said I'm sorry. Things got a little out of hand."

"But why? What got out of hand?"

With anybody else, the conversation would have been long over. But this was Mom. He couldn't shout at her. It was hard enough to still be hungover in front of her.

"It's just—that things are so out of hand out there. It just comes naturally. That feeling. Here, things are so nice and tidy. And last night I just forgot for a while and let myself go."

"You let yourself down," Mom said.

"Yeah, that too."

He felt her grip his hand. He couldn't believe the strength of that grip.

"You're stronger than that and we both know it."

He nodded.

"A lot of guys are looking at you. They're looking up to you. You need to be strong. For them. Because they don't know any better. You do."

March 23, 2008

Dear Mom:

First off I want to say sorry. I know I've already said this in person but it's different putting it in a letter. It feels more official, more concrete. I also just want to make sure you know that I am indeed sorry.

I'm not a kid anymore and you know that. I'm coming to you as someone who, as you said, knows better.

Sometimes it seems like this world is just so vicious. It bites and chews and spits out what it wants. The ugliness I've seen and heard about. Prayers are necessary, but sometimes I need more than silence in return. I can understand why guys need different things to cope, because there's a lot to cope with.

This reminded me about where my strength should ultimately come from. There are a lot of soldiers who are God-fearing men and women. It's not hard to find faith out there in the battlefield. I think it's actually easier, Mom. It's coming back home to indifference and apathy that makes faith start to wither away.

I'm sorry for letting you down, and I promise I won't do it again. Or I should say this—I promise that I'll try never to do it again. I'm not perfect and nobody is. All I can do is tell you that I've been served notice and I know it's time to start training to be sharp again.

See you on Sunday.

James

Beth

Sometimes the past chooses to show up on your front porch.

Sometimes you have no choice in the matter.

The snapshot is of Beth and James on the day before he left for Afghanistan. He is so big and so adult. James dwarfs her with an arm around her. They both smile.

Little did either of us know.

Then again, Beth knew. Something about this departure was different. It was different from the feeling she had when he left for training or when he left for Iraq.

She wonders now, looking at the photo and thinking back, if God perhaps nudged her. Or if a mother somehow knows.

The photo came out of the blue.

It came in the mail with a note. From her niece Dee, whose family lives in Asheville but who is currently attending college out in Colorado.

I found this on my digital camera and wasn't sure if you had it. I hope it was okay to send it. Thinking about and praying for you guys. Love, Dee

Hope it was okay.

This might be the last picture she has of the two of them.

To send or convey adequate thanks to her niece would be utterly impossible.

"What's that?"

The voice surprises her. Emily is there looking tanned and curious. Beth gives her the picture and the note.

"Such a great picture," Emily says. "He should've tried to go into the NFL instead of the army."

Beth notices a suitcase by the door. "Is it time?"

"Yeah."

"Want to stay for dinner?"

"Like you haven't seen enough of me?"

"One more meal won't hurt."

"I have plans. But thanks."

Emily gives her the picture back.

"You know, Mom, nobody needs to take our picture. I'm not going off to war like he did."

"I know."

"Maybe, but you sure don't *look* like you know."

"I'm sorry."

"We already talked about this."

"We did?" Beth asks.

"Well, we talked about it enough. I'm not going far away. Knoxville is only two hours away."

"I know."

"You sure? Sometimes I think you forget."

"Want me to drive you back up there?"

Emily shakes her head. She's so grown-up, so mature, so self-aware.

You blink and they're grown-up.

"Okay. Just give me a call when you get there."

"I will. Unless, of course, I pick up that crazy hitchhiker with the gun."

There are things she can say, things she probably should say, but instead Beth simply gives her daughter a hug.

Moments after Emily is gone, Beth finds the letter. The envelope was only sealed once and hasn't been opened. She holds it and wonders if it's time.

Yes, sometimes the past shows up unannounced.

Then again, sometimes the past remains tucked away, ignored and neglected.

Sometimes you do have a choice but simply refuse to make it.

Part Four

LETTERS FROM AFGHANISTAN

Beth

"It's okay."

"He needs to obey."

"I know that. But you don't need to worry so much."

"Yes I do. I don't want our four-year-old wandering around the neighborhood."

"Rich, it's fine. He's okay in our yard. You worry too much."

"There are ten thousand ways he can get hurt."

"There's only a dozen and you're just—honey, please. What is it? You're shaking."

"It's nothing."

"Tell me."

"James just wandered off and I thought I'd lost him."

"He's playing in the sandbox."

"He is now. But he was just—I ran around the house and for a minute I just thought the worst . . ."

"You always think the worst."

"When you've seen the worst you're inclined to think it."

"Listen. Look at me. He's okay. Rich, please, trust me. James is going to be fine. We need to do our job but we have to trust that God watches over him."

"I know."

"You don't act like you know."

"I just want to keep James and Emily inside, out of harm's way."

"You can't do that. You know that. They're not going to be four and two for the rest of their lives."

"Sometimes I wish they were."

"Your hands feel sweaty."

"I know."

"It's okay. Come here. Everything's fine."

———

Beth tries to remember the woman who spoke those words to her husband. She tries to remember being the woman who said that God watched over her children.

Even after James disappeared, that woman remained strong. But lately, the cracks in her armor have started to show.

Maybe it's my faith being challenged.

Another part of her doesn't think this has anything to do with her. This war and James's disappearance happened because there is evil in the world. This is one of those things that's difficult for a believer to explain. "Why did that tsunami hit?" "Where was God in the flooding of New Orleans?" "Why did He allow that earthquake to take so many lives in Haiti?"

Why do good people have to suffer?

Questions that can't and won't be answered, not in this world.

Evil and suffering and tragedy happen.

But when it knocks on your door, everything changes. When it barges into your house and sits down in your family room and decides to stay for a long while, you change.

It's inevitable.

She thinks of this after the call from Josie. Their eldest son, Matt, went to an ER last night because of a broken bone. Josie sounds relieved that it's nothing worse but also worn-out. Beth spent half an hour on the phone listening and encouraging her.

Now, as she contemplates something that she can do to help Josie, she can't help thinking of when the kids were younger.

He used to worry so much when they were little.

She wonders how Richard would have been as they got older. As the junior high years came and seemed to never end. As the teen years came.

Beth wonders if the strength that carried her through

those trying times somehow withered in this desert she's been passing through. Sometimes the days seem just like that—a caravan of one in an endless desert stuck under the piercing, needling sun.

Enough with the soul searching. It's time to make my friend some food.

As always, she knows work will carry her through to another day.

———

Josie looks tired and uncharacteristically casual in a sweatshirt and old jeans.

"How are you feeling today?" Beth asks as she puts the warm platter of lasagna sealed with tinfoil on top of Josie's oven.

"Beth, you didn't have to bring us dinner."

"Of course I did."

"Nobody died. It was just a broken bone."

"Still. I'm sure you've had a long day."

"Matt's the one feeling bad."

"Is he here?"

"Upstairs sleeping. You're going to be his hero if that's your lasagna."

"Wait," Beth jokes, "I thought he liked my broccoli casserole."

A few moments later, they're sharing a glass of wine and listening to music on the back deck. They've spent many hours in this backyard. The families grew up in each other's houses. Even after Richard passed away.

"Did I ever tell you about the time when James got sick as a dog and I had to take him to the ER?"

Josie looks tanned in the bath of afternoon sun. "When was that?"

"It was shortly after Richard died. I thought of that after you told me about Matt and his broken leg."

"What was wrong with James?"

"Just some virus. But he could not stop throwing up. He was so sick he could barely walk. He was just twelve or thirteen and he looked deathly pale. I remember being so angry that night."

"Angry at who?"

Beth stares out at the row of trees lining the back of the yard. "God."

Josie says a subdued "hmm" under her breath, letting her know she gets it.

"Grandma had stayed to watch Emily. It was two in the morning because the ER on a Saturday night was beyond busy. I needed to get a prescription for antinausea pills for James, and I just—everything exploded that night. In the parking lot of a Walgreens. I had a meltdown."

"That's understandable."

"I was so furious. And I walked around with the

same fury for months after Richard died. Outwardly I was fine."

"Not really. You weren't fooling everybody."

"I know. But I figured I was fooling most. But I wasn't fooling God. And I was so mad. I wanted—I demanded to know why. Why leave me alone? Why leave me to take care of things like this all on my own? I screamed and I wept. I pounded on my steering wheel."

"Sometimes you have to do that. That or open a bottle of wine."

"You want to hear the end of that story?"

"Is there an end?" Josie asks.

"There was an end to that chapter, at least. And it was when you gave me that key ring. The one with the carving of the mustard seed."

"That's right. I forgot. Do you still have that?"

"No. Well, not really. I gave it to James on the day he went to basic training. And I told him the same thing you told me. 'If you have faith even as small as a mustard seed, you can say to this mountain, "Move from here to there," and it will move. Nothing will be impossible.'"

"I found that ugly little key ring at a garage sale. You know that?"

"The gift came right after I jumped into the ring to take on God."

"We always lose when we do that."

Beth looks at the woman across from her. "I've kept

that verse and that gift in the back of my mind and my heart, Josie. That's why I still believe. That's why I refuse to give up on James."

"So I'm to blame for your having hope?"

"Hope is a beautiful and blessed thing. How can it not be? I have to remind myself of that. Daily. And things like that—your finding a little key ring at a garage sale and giving it to me at the most meaningful time I could have had it—I don't believe they're accidental. And I pray—I pray all the time for one thing."

"What is that?"

"I pray I'll get it back. That James will come home and give it to me. He won't have to say anything. We'll both know what it means."

Josie smiles and takes her hand. "I pray you never lose that faith, Beth. That's the best thing about you, the thing I've always admired. I'm sorry for asking—for even suggesting—that you stop that. Maybe it's just because I've struggled to have it myself."

"We all struggle. We just do it in our own ways."

James

March 18, 2009

Dear Mom:

And so I start my first letter from Afghanistan. It's exciting to be writing to you from here. It's amazing to think that nine months ago I was on my honeymoon. Now I'm back at war.

It's been a couple weeks now, and thankfully our unit hasn't come across any heavy enemy activity. We remain ready to fight at any moment. The sounds of gunfire and bombs remind us we're in a combat zone. Thankfully the enemy fire on our locations hasn't resulted in many injuries.

The guys are excited and motivated. I can't speak for other units, but our guys are eager to serve.

The company has been training, taking inventories, and planning construction projects. There's a road project we're working on along with building some things over here. We're also continuing to work alongside the Afghan army to keep training them.

The country over here is breathtaking, Mom. The mountain ranges are really rugged, making the weather totally different in spots that are close to each other. Hiking in them can be treacherous, but it's worth the view.

Do you want to know something funny? I still have that mustard seed key ring. I carry it with me every day. Every time I feel it or think about it, I remember what it stands for.

A nice little glimmer of hope is good and necessary, because you never know when you're going to need it the most.

Take care of yourself and that beautiful wife of mine. Love you all and talk soon.

                                                    James

———

She walks with Richie down the sidewalk holding his little hand. With each day, he reminds Beth more of his father.

Life is a gift, she thinks. *That sweet little touch is a gift.*

In the stark sunlight, this is what she chooses to accept. This is what she tells herself. Even though fall has come and Emily has gone off to school and the two-year anniversary is nearly here, Beth chooses to accept the blessings she has.

Sure it might be work.

But I have to give thanks to the Lord, for I know He is good and His faithful love will remain forever.

The shadows stretch out, showing Grandma and the little figure beside her.

Beth thinks of his father.

Some wandered in the desert lost and homeless. Hungry and thirsty, they nearly died.

Beth thinks of the faraway land he ended up lost in.

He rescued them from their distress.

The words of the psalm that greeted her this morning are brighter than the sun above, more vibrant than the colors starting to work their way onto the trees, more real than that tiny hand in hers.

She thinks of Psalm 107 and knows that she could

live off that alone. So much encouragement and wisdom.

Those who are wise will take all this to heart; they will see in our history the faithful love of the Lord.

In clear moments on days like this, with her one grandson at her side, Beth knows that God is near. These moments are what help her get through the sunsets, when the melancholy moon hangs above, her grandson's hand no longer there to hold on to, and the psalmist begins to lament the dark night to come.

"Grandma?"

The voice sings to her.

"You okay?" she asks Richie.

"Uh-huh."

"What is it? Are you hungry?"

"Uh-huh."

"Me too. Let's make the biggest peanut butter sandwich you've ever seen."

"Big?"

"No. *This* big."

On the drive home from babysitting Richie, Beth decides to make the phone call. Despite her misgivings.

Someone answers on the second ring.

"You win," Beth says.

"Hey. I was just thinking of you."

Emily doesn't sound distant or busy. She sounds as if she might be sitting across from her on the couch watching HGTV.

"I couldn't," Beth says.

"You couldn't what?"

"I couldn't last a week."

Emily laughs. "It's fine."

The important things in life are the normal things. Not vacations to the Grand Canyon or the Grand Cayman Islands. Not buying a new car or birthday presents or a graduation gift. It's not the big moments that count but the small. The big moments are the exclamation points on the sentences that have come before them.

"How are things going?"

"I shaved my head and got a couple of tattoos."

"Very funny."

"Mom—I haven't been gone long enough to know how things are going."

"Okay."

"Wait—oh, is that my cue to ask you how things are going on your end?"

"I was just thinking today that we should've done more this summer. Perhaps I should've gone to that concert you went to."

"You said you hated that music."

"Well, like I said, you're right," Beth states. "You win."

"Did we bet anything? Like maybe an iPad?"

"Not exactly."

"Mom, I'm not trying to win anything."

Beth pauses for a moment. "I'm sorry."

"About what?"

"About this summer. About the way I handled things."

"It's okay," Emily says.

"I've been thinking—this whole week—that maybe it's time."

"Time for what?"

She knows Emily understands.

"Mom . . ."

"I think you've been right. You've been right all along."

"Mom, please—"

"I just think it's time. I'm ready to move on. Ready to stop putting my life on hold."

"Is he?"

"I think James would have wanted me to move on long before now."

"Mom, don't."

"Don't what?"

"Don't give up. Just wait."

Beth sighs. *First Josie, now Emily. Everybody wants me to keep hope alive, even those who have questioned it.*

"I don't understand. You're contradicting yourself," Beth responds.

"I'm a college student," Emily says. "I'm allowed to do that."

"I still don't understand."

"I think it's easier being able to think the way I do knowing you believe that James is still out there. I feel like if *you* stop believing and hoping and praying, then he really will be gone."

Beth sighs. "So what's that mean?"

"I don't know. I guess it means I'm tired of trying to think about what it means. Sometimes I start thinking about him and then I just . . ." Emily lets out a groan. "I can't. I can't do this drama, not tonight."

"But you were just telling me—"

"I know. But you just need to do what you need to do."

"Em?"

"I have to go."

"Did I say something?"

"No. I did. And I probably said way too much."

There is something precious about a toddler falling to sleep while being read to. Tonight Grandma got Richie to bed by reading several of his favorite books. Just

short ones with lots of colors and definitions, ones Beth
reads over and over again.

When she comes back into the family room, Beth is
surprised by a question from Britt.

"Do you think James knew he wasn't going to come
back?"

"Why?"

"Sometimes I think he knew. Maybe it's just me.
Maybe it's what any couple goes through—doubts and
fears and everything."

"Did something happen?"

Britt shakes her head. "I never showed you the letter
he sent me right before he left for Afghanistan. It wasn't
his last letter, but in some ways it might have been."

"What did it say?"

Britt stands up and leaves the kitchen, then comes
back carrying an envelope. The light sounds of
instrumental music fill the still evening surrounding
them.

"I've thought about this so much. After everything
we were talking about—I still don't know if it would be
right or wrong to move on. But—well, read the letter."

Beth opens it and finds the familiar scrawl she loves.

February 28, 2009

Dear Britt:

I'm sorry about last night. I don't know why it's so easy for me to do some things in life and so hard to do other things. I can stand in front of an enemy and, without fear or hesitation, shoot and kill him. Yet I can't stand before my own expecting wife and share with her my thoughts and feelings. It's just always been easier for me to write them.

When we were at Olive Garden and then afterward at the movie—before when we were just sitting there and then on the ride home—all that time I wanted to say this.

If something ever happens to me, I understand that you need to go on. I not only understand it, but I demand that things go on. Not just for you but for our child. I don't want you putting your life on hold any more than you already have. I don't want you to wait, Britt. I don't want you to be stuck in a pool of grief. I don't want you hanging on last words and broken promises and pictures from yesterday.

I learned after my father passed away that you can't live in yesterday. You can't live in tomorrow, either. But you can plan for tomorrow by living in today. By living in the now.

The thought of leaving the two of you alone . . . I just

can't talk about it. There's something about saying things out loud that makes them seem so much more concrete and real.

I believe that if I die in duty, it's God's will. And I also believe that you will be able to allow someone else to fall for you the same way I fell for you. You are too precious not to be loved every moment of every day of the rest of your life. And all I ask—the very thing I wanted to ask of you last night—is that you don't wait. Don't keep yourself from moving on.

I don't like wallowing in the fears and the maybes of life. That's why this is so hard. I don't like thinking this way. I like thinking of our grandchildren and us vacationing in Europe and what it's going to be like the next time I make love to you. I don't like thinking about good-byes.

But I say this because I have to. So if there's anything of mine you keep, if there are any words that you remember, remember these:

It's okay to move on.

It's not only okay. It's necessary.

I want you to promise me that you will remember this and do it if you have to.

And I promise you I will do my best to keep you from ever having to fulfill this promise.

I love you.

Talk soon.

James

Beth folds the letter and looks at her daughter-in-law. "What did you tell him?"

"I told him I would," Britt says. "I promised. And all this time, I've been questioning whether or not I've been breaking that promise. Because I don't want to move on. I'm still not ready. Even on nights when Richie is unbearable and I feel like I can't do this by myself, I can't picture being with anybody else."

"I know."

"I'm afraid I'll never be ready. I don't know when it will happen, Beth. And that's the most terrifying thought—that'll I'll always be like this. Always."

For a moment, Beth lets the silence linger like a puff of smoke hanging in the room.

"You know who you're talking to, don't you?"

Britt looks at her, unsure what Beth is referring to.

"Some people have suggested that I 'move on.' Like it's as easy as changing addresses. And no, I'm not talking about with James. I'm talking about with my husband. With Richard."

"What did they say?"

"I heard everything. Clichés like 'There are other fish in the sea.' Truths like 'It's okay to let go of his memory.' But the truth is this—I've never wanted to find someone to replace him. There is no replacing a love like that. There have been men where I thought, yes, sure, they might be a really good husband. But I've never allowed myself to go down that road."

"Do you regret it?"

"No," Beth says quickly. "Never."

"I feel like that letter holds the last words I'll ever hear from James."

"I can understand that. Richard left us all letters to read after he passed away."

"What did yours say?"

"I don't know. I still haven't opened mine. I'm waiting for the right time."

James

May 14, 2009

Dear Mom:

There are walking casualties, Mom, the kind the media seldom reports about, the kind few of us want to acknowledge.

I'm a newlywed in my marriage, but when it comes to the army, I feel like a veteran. I feel aged and toned and ready. I'm sad to say, however, that not all of my brothers end up this way.

Some go home from the war but never leave it behind. For some, the war wages on in their souls and soon takes them to their eternal home.

The doctors call it post-traumatic stress disorder. I call it something else: It's the enemy waging war on the home front. It's the devil wreaking havoc with men and their families and friends.

I'd be the same, Mom, without my faith. My faith provides crutches even though I still hobble around.

There was a guy I knew in Iraq. His name was Ted Seybert but everybody just called him Bert. He was a decent guy, levelheaded, not one known for violent outbursts. You fall in line and do what you're supposed to do. When your sergeant tells you to hit anything moving, you hit anything moving. You shout a loud "hoo-ah" and do what you're told. You don't hesitate and you don't think twice afterward.

But still, the mind remembers. Your heart can't forget. We're not wired to hurt and kill and when we do, we remember. That's why the nightmares come. That's why sometimes it feels like our unit in Iraq was a psychiatric ward with a bunch of guys being prescribed pocketfuls of antidepressants and sleeping pills.

Bert wasn't one of those guys needing the pills or the booze and pot to get by. But something happened on his way back to the States.

I saw him not long ago when I was back home.

Not long before he killed himself.

The things he'd seen—the things we'd all seen—it's impossible not to be affected by them. But I also think different people are strong in different areas. It's not just my faith that's kept me grounded and out of harm's way emotionally. It's been my family too, and my ability to compartmentalize. And avoiding bad habits.

They slip up on you, the bad habits. For a while I'd get drunk with the guys and it felt so easy, Mom. I always thought, I'm not doing anything else wrong. I felt like I needed the alcohol because of what I was facing all the time. But then I realized it only made me weaker and more prone to trouble. Habits are hard to break. It's one thing to need to drink out there in the darkness, but it's another to need to do so when I'm with my own bride.

Britt knows all this—we talk about it. I can compartmentalize but she needs to know.

But Bert's death—it's hard for me to fathom how the guy who stayed so levelheaded amid days of worrying about being blown to shreds could stick a gun in his mouth and fire away.

I'm glad that the news reports good things, because there are lots of good things to report.

But there are tragedies happening every day. And there are the walking wounded, the soldiers who are physically fine but mentally and emotionally gone.

I pray for them. I pray for their families.

I pray that I can do something for them.

I pray and thank God that I'm not one of them.

It's by His grace, Mom.

It's by His grace that I'm still here, that I'm still alive, that I'm walking only partially wounded.

Maybe Dad's death showed me that anything can happen, that I have to be able to keep going no matter what. He told me to take my sadness over his death and do something positive with it. And I tried to do that. Thinking about Bert, I'm still trying to do that, every day.

I not only value your prayers, Mom, but I need them. Along with the assurance of my faith, they are what keep me upright.

Thank you.

Talk soon. One day (and don't give me a hard time for this), we have to Skype each other. Though it does require turning on a computer, which I know can sometimes be a chore for you. ☺

Love you,
James

Beth

"I make the best meatball in the world."

Beth makes a *tsk* sound with her tongue. "Don't make fun of me."

"I'm not," Marion says.

"Just because you're Italian means you're supposed to make good meatballs, right? So I'm to believe."

"It's true. Ask any of my boys. Or look at my husband. He's the body to prove it."

"What's your secret?"

"Oh, no. I can't tell. Not even you."

"I promise I won't reveal your recipe."

"Oh, no. Family secret. Blood was lost over those instructions."

"Seriously?"

"No." Marion chuckles.

It's been half an hour and not once have the boys

been mentioned. Beth finds it refreshing that the broken record hasn't been played, at least not so far.

Perhaps Marion doesn't share this sentiment.

"It's going to be two years in two days. Have you thought of that?"

"Of course."

"I wish I could come fly down and see you. But that's going to be a busy time for me at work. Maybe the following week?"

"I should be coming up there to see you."

"We have to visit New York if you do. That Francisco—oh how he loves the city."

"James always wanted to buy a big ranch with lots of property."

"I can just hear them now, talking about stuff like that. It's amazing to think of, boys like that from different walks of life, from such different families, becoming closer than brothers."

Or women like that from different parts of the country and different lives becoming closer than sisters.

"Thank you," Beth says.

"For what?"

"For these calls."

"Please. It's my therapy. You're the only sane person I know. If you met my family, you'd realize why I call."

"Still, it means a lot. You've always been the proactive one."

"My husband would say 'overbearing.'"

"Sometimes we need a little 'overbearing' in our lives."

"That's right," Marion says. "I'm going to quote you next time the family is over for Sunday lunch."

"I want to come."

"Anytime. You just walk in any time you want to."

———

Anything can happen.

Those words go through her mind as her night suddenly changes in dramatic fashion.

It starts with the ringing of the phone. It's Professor Diephouse, Emily's English professor whom they met on their first visit to the university. He's wondering if there's a reason why she's missed a week of classes without a call or an e-mail alerting him as to why.

"I have no idea," Beth tells the professor. Her heart is pounding.

As an English major, Emily had talked about her favorite professor often. He looked like a modern-day version of William Faulkner.

"Usually I wouldn't call a student's home. But these days—with a girl like Emily . . . she's never struck me as someone who would casually blow off a week of classes."

"She's not."

The panic is bubbling over.

"I don't mean to make you worry, Mrs. Thompson."

She thinks about the last time she spoke with Emily. It's been a week.

"I just thought—"

"No, thank you," she says. "I will find out what's going on."

It takes only a few seconds to dial her daughter. She tries three times and gets her voice mail three times.

The panic is no longer bubbling. It's bleeding into her.

But these days—with a girl like Emily . . .

Beth knows what he's talking about. Pretty young girls like Emily make the news for all the wrong reasons. For all the reasons that make the world a scary place, that make mothers have to truly live by faith alone, that test their ability to let them go.

Lord, please, let Emily be okay.

She's prayed like that twice, only to have the floodgates break twice. The day Richard told her he had cancer. And the day the men came to her door to tell her that James had gone missing.

Now this.

In these days of instant everything, she can't find a way to get hold of Emily. There's no phone to her dorm room, and Beth can't find her roommate's number.

Calm down, Beth. Everything's going to be okay.

She recalls the professor's words.

But these days.

She tries to call Emily again, only to leave another voice mail. Then she calls Josie to get someone else's opinion.

Beth can barely get the words out.

"We don't know anything for sure, so let's just wait," Josie says.

"It's almost ten at night and she should be answering her phone. She's skipped classes all week. Do you know what that means?"

Josie tells her that she's coming over.

Beth tries calling Emily again. Once again, there's nothing.

So let's just wait.

Let's . . . just . . . wait.

Beth gets her keys and storms into the garage.

She's tired of waiting.

Her whole life has been waiting. Waiting for word. Waiting for the knock on the door. Waiting to get a phone call. Waiting for an e-mail. Waiting for a letter. Waiting to read, words to hear, to know, to understand, to find out.

She curses and starts the car and almost forgets to press open the garage door.

Enough waiting.

Enough not knowing.

She can't breathe she's hurting so much.

Not Emily, Lord, not my little girl, not the only one left.

As she pulls out onto the street and drives toward the freeway, Beth turns on the radio, hoping it will calm her nerves.

The university is not very far away and if Emily doesn't answer her phone, then she'll find Emily. It doesn't matter where she is or what state she's in; Beth is going to find her baby.

———

Where are You? Do You hear me? Do You, God?

She wants to scream out loud. The highway is dark like her heart, the road empty and endless. She speeds and dares a cop to stop her. She dares God to answer.

I've been patient and I've been waiting and I've been asking over and over and over again but nothing. Nothing but silence.

Her hands are strangling the steering wheel, the rest of her body rigid.

What have I done to You? Why, Lord?

The fury swells with the storm, the raging winds and the bellowing waves bubbling over. Beth knows she should probably slow down or better yet, pull over and get out of the car. Maybe walk off her steam. Last thing she should be doing is driving in a state of mindless rage.

Every time she thinks of something happening to Emily, her thoughts turn to James and then Richard and then poor, woeful, pitiful Beth. *Woe is me driving the car. Woe is me driving without knowing the full story, without waiting.*

And, of course, without bringing her cell phone.

She knows that Emily might have already been calling and she might be fine.

Yet Beth is trying to outrace God and time and destiny and fate and everything.

You can't, Beth.

Eventually her arms and legs relax, she slows the car, and she cools down.

She's starting now to breathe in and breathe out, taking measured breaths the way she did when she had both of her children.

Beth switches the radio channel. One of her favorite artists is singing an appropriate song.

The piano and the chords and the verses and the voice all soothe her.

They wash over her like aloe over a sunburn.

The words are being sung for her, for an audience of one.

The words and the story move her. *Joy. Love. Hallelujah. Thank you.*

She sighs and lets her body and her soul relax as the highway continues to stretch out.

God is love.

She knows this but needs this triumphant reminder.

He is love.

She can't do it on her own and she isn't expected to.

Beth turns down the radio and asks God to watch over her and her family and her daughter. She asks God for forgiveness, then thanks Him. Her heart stops racing. She acknowledges that He is in control, despite those fears and needs and those deep roots of pain.

The worry is still there. It doesn't magically disappear. But she can breathe steadily and know that whatever she's going to find out on campus, she will find with Someone by her side.

⸺

Some say life is random and meaningless. That prayers are worthless and drift off into silence.

Some say and believe that.

But when Beth manages to finally get to Emily's dorm room after getting lost several times on campus and then asking a couple of girls to let her in the dorm, she thinks otherwise.

Emily is there with her roommates. Beth breaks up the casual conversation and rushes in to hug her daughter. She embraces her in a way she hasn't done for years. It's a hug of relief, of desperation, of fear.

"Uh, Mom?"

When Beth finally lets her go, Emily is totally perplexed.

"When was the last time you checked your phone?"

When she says that, the other girls in the room laugh.

"Yeah. Well—that's a little problem," Emily says.

"What?"

"I sorta think I lost it."

"You lost your phone? Where?"

"*That's* the question. I was trying to figure out a way to tell you I'd lost it. Especially after hounding you all that time to let me buy it."

"Em—your professor called me and said you hadn't been to class for a week?"

"Come on. Why don't we head outside, okay?"

Beth has gone from furious with worry to furious with frustration in just a matter of minutes.

Such is the life of any mother.

———

They're sitting in the back of a coffee shop that's open twenty-four hours. Emily hasn't said much since they walked over here to talk.

"Em, what's going on?"

"Nothing's wrong. Okay? I mean, I'm not pregnant or in trouble with the law and I haven't been kidnapped by al-Qaeda."

"Stop it."

"I'm fine. Besides my new iPhone being lost. That nearly killed me."

"Why would you skip classes for a week?"

"Because I'm thinking of dropping out."

For a while, Beth can't think of anything to say.

Of all the things she thought she might hear tonight, this is not one of them.

"Why? Why in the world would you want to do something like that?"

"It's not that I *want* to. It's just—I can't really sum it up exactly."

"Why don't you try?" Beth says.

"Don't be all annoyed."

"I'm more than annoyed."

"I just don't know what I want. What I *should* want. I mean—a big part of the reason I'm even going here is because of Dad. Because it was always about University of Tennessee. He's not even here to see me attending. And neither is James."

"You wanted to come here."

"I don't know what I want. I just—want a break."

"A break? Didn't you just have one this summer?"

"No. I mean a break. A break to figure out where I'm going. What I'm supposed to do."

"I don't get it."

Emily nods and scratches at the side of the coffee

cup she hasn't even touched. "Everybody has their place in our family. Dad knew what he was all about. So did James. You're the mother of James and the grandmother of Richie. Even Britt is something. She has her identity. But me—what am I? Or who am I? I've spent my entire life around people who know who they are."

"Me? Who am I?"

"An army wife. A mom. A grandmother." Emily continues. "All along, I've wondered who I'm supposed to be. I've even wondered if I should join the army."

"You have not."

"I've never told you or James but I think—well, should I? I mean, everybody else has found their destiny. What about mine?"

"You're twenty-one. You don't have to find it right away."

"Dad discovered it, right? So did James."

"Some people spend their whole life trying to find an identity. You're so young. You'll find it."

"Some people I've known have gone looking for it. They've taken a break."

"That's just ridiculous," Beth says. "Why would you do this suddenly? Why now?"

"I've been thinking about this all summer. It's just— you've been pretty occupied with other things."

It's true.

Emily goes on. "And it's okay. Mom—it's okay. I get

it. I would be doing a lot worse if I was in your shoes."

"You are in my shoes."

"No. It's different. I can't really understand what you're going through. I've tried but I can't."

"Em, I'm sorry. For not being there this summer. For being so busy."

"It's fine."

"No, it's not. I was so scared that something happened to you tonight."

"I'm fine."

"I didn't know that. I was terrified."

"I'm sorry."

"You have to tell me these things."

"Like the lost phone?"

Beth grabs her daughter's hand. "Like the lost place in life. You need to let me know."

"That's what I'm doing now, right?"

"I'm sorry it took me this long to listen."

"I'm just trying to figure out what's next, you know?"

As Beth nods her head, she realizes that it's about time that she does the same.

James

June 12, 2009

Dear Mom:

I know you've wondered why I came back out for a second term when I could be back with Britt and the rest of you. I know that it's more than simply being bored or restless. When buddies of mine at home were complaining about the BMW they couldn't buy or bragging about their recent drunken brawl, I knew it was time. But it was more than that.

I needed to come back out here to find meaning.

I know that I'm doing more good here than back at home punching a time clock. I know you feel that I'll make a good father. But I can be a good father by leading by example.

I want my son or daughter to know that their father was doing what he felt best when they were born: serving his country.

The longer I'm out here, the more I realize that it's the small moments of life that count.

The touch of cool water against the tongue. The taste of a steak hot off the grill. The sound of birds in the backyard.

Whether they are luxuries that I'm afforded over here or memories from home that I'm awakened with, I think I'm really learning what life is all about.

I think of the infinitesimal freedoms and luxuries we take for granted. I think of those every day I'm over here.

I believe I'm meant to be here, right here, for a reason. I just can't say exactly what that reason is except to serve and protect.

Love you,
James

Beth

Maybe it's time to stop waiting and wondering and believing.

Maybe I've put life on hold.

Maybe I've been busy and have avoided living. Maybe I've been outrunning life and responsibilities.

Maybe I've lost my identity, too.

Maybe his body and his soul are at rest and it's time for me to do the same—to put to rest all the questions and wondering and hoping.

Maybe James never made it after saving Corporal Jesse Burks.

Maybe he died in a hole from starvation. Otherwise, why wouldn't he be displayed and forced to talk to a camera to renounce the war?

Maybe James was strong and resisted speaking out. Maybe he got shot or decapitated doing so.

Maybe James lost his mind.

Maybe he escaped only to wander around in the foothills of a place vaguely resembling hell. Maybe he managed to get to a safe place only to realize he was stuck and couldn't go anywhere else.

Maybe he's watching me now, all alone in a cloud of doubt, wondering what he can do to make things easier.

Maybe James is throwing a football with Richard in heaven.

Maybe that idea is better suited to a birthday card than to dwelling inside of my mind.

Maybe it's time I stop with all the maybes of life and get to the things I know and can do.

⸻

"I saw James yesterday."

For a second, Beth leaves the fork in the mashed potatoes. "You saw James? Where?"

Between her and Britt, there is enough food on the table for a family of six. Maybe that's one of those subconscious things, something that a counselor would analyze with some deep, pithy meaning. For Beth, it's a habit that started when she married and then had two children. Some habits aren't hard to break. Some habits she doesn't want to break.

"On the sidewalk. Right in front of me. Wearing his military garb. Walking like nothing was wrong."

There has to be a punch line and Beth waits.

"I called out his name and actually ran to him. I *ran*. Can you believe it? And the poor man, who really looked nothing like James—I was so embarrassed when I went up and grabbed him. I couldn't say a word."

"So you didn't tell him?"

Britt laughs, her eyes sad and amused at the same time. "Other people were looking at us. I just felt so pathetic."

"I'm sorry."

There it goes, another meal half finished. Beth's appetite has vanished again.

"I swear, for a brief moment I thought it was him."

Beth notices the freckles on Britt's nose and cheeks. Even though Richie takes so much after his father, he still has reminders of his mother, like the handful of freckles.

"Is it always going to be like this?"

"No," Beth says.

"Are you sure?"

"You remember those first few weeks with Richie? Maybe the first few months?"

"They were kind of a blur."

"I remember so many people telling me after I had Emily that things were going to get better. The sleep deprivation, the long days and the longer nights, the fussiness that never seemed to go away. Times when I'd be alone and I'd just wonder if *this* was my life. It eventually got easier."

"But do you think this ever will?" Britt asks with a sigh.

"I promise you, sweetie. Life isn't going to always be on hold. It can't be."

"Some of the stories I've heard. Wives who have moved on and then discovered their husbands alive. I just can't . . ."

"I know."

Britt stares down at her plate. "I'm sorry."

"Don't be."

"I shouldn't have said anything."

"Yes, you should. You can say anything to me."

"Sometimes I think that when James went missing over there, a part of me went missing too."

I know, sweetheart, I know and I understand and if I could I'd do anything to help. I would.

"I just want that part back," Britt says. "Even if James never comes home, I want to find that part of me again."

September 20, 2011

Dear Britt,

Just a little note to say keep hanging in there. Keep praying. I'm continuing to pray for you and want to share something from my Bible study today.

I've grown up listening to Psalm 23. "The Lord is my shepherd, I shall not want." But today, I learned something new.

Near the end, it says, "You prepare a table before me in the presence of my enemies. You anoint my head with oil; my cup overflows."

I've never quite thought of the anointing-the-head-with-oil-and-overflowing-cup part of this verse. I just thought it was symbolic. The anointing of the head with oil symbolizes baptism. The overflowing cup symbolizes God's overflowing love.

But I discovered that there's more to this.

My Bible study says that a shepherd taking care of his sheep would examine his flock to make sure none of them were badly injured from the day. If they were, he would apply oil to their wounds, along with providing them water from a cup. The oil would also be placed on the sheep's head and horns in order to keep the insects away.

We're the sheep in this passage, Britt. Obviously. And the Shepherd is meticulous in taking care of his flock.

It's not just knowing that the Shepherd is nearby when

the dark valleys come. It's not just the realization that His rod and staff will protect and comfort.

He really, truly takes care of us. He searches us for wounds we might have gotten throughout the course of a day. He brings us salve for them.

We are promised a house to live in with Him forever. We're not in the forever part just yet, so we have to make it through each day looking for His comfort and care.

Just don't forget the Great Shepherd is there.

I love you and will see you soon.

Beth

James

Dear Mom:

The world is mean, Mom. It's mean and it's empty. Sometimes it's the paths I find myself walking on. Sometimes it's the stories I hear the men sharing. Sometimes it's the things I find myself having to do. War isn't just in this country. It's in our hearts, too.

I remember once asking Dad why God allowed him to get cancer. And if God was going to allow him to die. And he said that this world was broken, all of it and all of us. And that God wasn't going to fix it right away. That was why people got sick. Or why people waged war. Sin and suffering went hand in hand, and it was because the whole thing got broken right after it was created.

For years I've carried that around, wondering what he meant.

I've seen so many happy things, so many good things.

Amazing and awesome sights to behold. But I've also learned that Dad was right. This place is broken.

So am I.

It's amazing what we can do to each other. What we as humans have done and will do. I know these aren't the words you're probably wanting to hear today, Mom. I'm sorry. I know I should be talking about the troops and how we're fixing things. But I can't. I just find it hard to believe that God doesn't just get sick of us all and wipe us out.

"He's going to fix us one day," Dad said. "And the broken pieces are going to be put back together."

There won't be any more of this. This fighting. This danger. This destruction.

I dream of that day.

I know we're the ones who messed this thing up. It's not God's fault. It's by His grace that we're able to live at all.

I thought I'd be stronger, to tell the truth. The biggest thing broken is me. I pray daily for God to mend me as much as possible so I can help others who are hurting and in need.

Sometimes I can't wait to get home, but home scares me. I know it's going to let me down in some ways because even it is broken. I've met guys who have gone back only to want—to need—to come back out here. The thought of that—especially after coming home to our little baby girl or boy—is crazy. But I also know that I have to temper my expectations. It's going to take time to adjust back to that life.

There's this line from the movie The Thin Red Line that I have written in my journal: "The tough part is not knowing if you're doing any good. That's the hard part."

I think about that all the time, wonder if I'm doing any good whatsoever. I don't know.

Meaning is something I'm still searching for, to be honest. But it'll come. I gotta believe it will come.

I love you.
James

Beth

Gerald Stewart Murphy was a soldier.

He was born just another boy on January 21, 1927, but he died on September 24, 2011, a decorated marine.

When they wrote his bio, they didn't share what he thought of the Korean War. They didn't describe his struggles over going there in the first place or the tragedies that befell him when he came back.

They simply said that he served his country.

There was no color commentary, no battle story, no explanation of the war itself or its place in history.

Gerald Stewart Murphy, Beth's friend from the Mountain Home VAMC, is remembered as a veteran and a hero and a man with an unyielding spirit and an unpredictable tongue. Yet those fellow soldiers who served alongside him said he provided one of the most blessed things he could while serving in a foreign country.

Humor.

So many years later, Murphy hadn't changed much except for growing older and more cynical.

Beth sits in church with Emily at her side. They listen to the stories of two men who served with Murphy, along with a young woman who talks about her grandfather.

But the thing that moves Beth the most is when Murphy's daughter reads a letter he wrote from Korea.

Of course when she simply hears the word "letter," she perks up and listens extra close.

It's as if God is speaking in His own unique way.

"My father wrote this letter in April 1952 shortly before getting wounded and coming home," the middle-aged woman says. "It was sent to my mom and it was something she passed along to me. Dad never knew I had it. My mom didn't want to bring up the war. But I share this to give a little insight into the man my father was—how loving, and how damaged by war."

Dear Ruth:

Something in me tells me that I'm not going to be here much longer. I don't mean to be so pessimistic at the start of this letter, but I know you. I know you'd sniff it out even if I didn't state it right away. You know me, even 6,500 miles away while I'm writing in a place that rhymes with Bang Dang Dong.

I miss you something fierce. I miss your nagging. Because at least I get to sleep with that nagging voice and get a chance to hear you stop nagging. Sometimes silence is my worst enemy, because silence means I'm alone.

This is a place of nightmares. It's the wandering around that just goes on and on. It's the insensitivity. You lose a little of caring bit by bit as you navigate through hell. I think that's what hell is like if it exists—a place where all sensitivity has been jettisoned and you're left with savages.

I carry that picture you sent. You and Gloria are so beautiful. I carry it close and don't show a soul because I want to keep you all for myself.

I imagine all those who get to see your sweet face on a daily basis. It makes me jealous. I think of Gloria and how she's growing and what I'm missing.

I try not to question why I'm here. That gets you nowhere. I just try to remind myself that I'm still human and that I still have a soul and that maybe I'm helping out. I'm doing the right thing. I was asked to come and I'm over here.

Fighting? Not really. Sometimes. More like wandering and searching and being shot at in distant cities but not really fighting.

I don't think these people have any idea about the kind of freedom that picture of yours brings to mind. You and Gloria on the swing on the back porch. I can smell something wonderful in the kitchen and hear the birds. Those sorts of things don't exist over here. These people are ghosts, their joys depleted. It's all wrong. This fight, the deaths, the long nights. The crazy sense of nothing over here.

I think of you two and I remain thankful for living in a good country. We're helping out, right? That's what I'm told. That's what soldiers do.

I want to make it home and feel you in my arms and feel my daughter in my arms. I want to sit on the swing with the two of you. I want to hear the sounds of dogs barking in the background without explosions following. I want to see the sunset and then listen to my records and then fall asleep with you.

You don't know how good you can have it until you see the underbelly.

The sun rises and sets on you two.

If there's a way, I'll be coming home back to both of you.

I love you.
Murphy

This could be any husband talking to any wife.

Any soldier talking to his family.

Any daughter reading any letter written by her father.

The words are familiar and haunting and break Beth's heart.

She also realizes that these words were written by a man almost sixty years ago.

The only difference is that Murphy never held on to the hope Beth holds.

Murphy said if there was a way, he was coming back home to both of them. And Murphy, God rest his soul, did come home.

Let it be the same for James, Lord. Please let it be the same.

<hr />

At first, she is unsure.

It's not that Beth hasn't ridden a horse in her life. Of course she has. But it's been so long. And her body, forty-four on the outside, isn't quite keeping up with the twentysomething spirit that she feels on the inside—today.

The Palomino walking horse strides with confidence and utter calm. Beth loves the feel of this big creature underneath her, the steady stride of its legs, the light

cream mane and tail. Beth loves the way Misty moves
without a care in the world.

The day is cooler, the sky dabbed with white, the
glow of autumn all around. Beth follows Josie at a
leisurely pace, forgetting what time of day it is, forgetting
what day it is. Forgetting most everything.

Yet she doesn't forget how thankful she is.

This is what heaven must feel like.

Not like some magical fairy tale where she rides a
white unicorn. The grip of the leather saddle and the
crunch of the horse's hooves on gravel are as real as
they should be. But there is no fear. With every step that
Misty takes, Beth is slowly letting go.

*Heaven is a place without any wars or rumors of wars.
There will be no hate and no arguments and no fighting
and no end to the eternal peace.*

"You doing okay?"

And for the first time in some time, Beth believes
she is.

She's already forgotten the trail they've crossed over.
She just wants to see what's ahead. With the grace
and the assurance of this blessed creature. So calm. So
soothing.

*I'm not leaving you, James. I will never leave you and
you know that. But I have to see what's up ahead. I must
see what's around the corner.*

"We're going downhill but she's a pro, so don't worry!"

She waves at Josie and then strokes Misty's silky mane.

She's not worried.

Not anymore.

James

Dear Mom:

He will never again sit on a couch and cheer on his favorite football team in glorious high definition.

He won't be able to taste a cold beer after cutting the grass at the end of a hot summer day.

He won't ever hear the sounds of his own children playing in that backyard, swinging on a swing set and sliding down a slide.

He will never sit in church on a cool fall morning, his family and friends surrounding him.

Fred Lewis died in the dust of another land. He fell in a street without a name. He died so that we are able to sit on that couch and drink that beer and hear those children and go to that church.

The luxuries we—I—take for granted.

It's not just that we take our homes and jobs and friends

for granted, Mom. It's our lives. It's the moon watching over us at night. It's the assurance of the rising sun.

Every day we live here knowing it might be our last. We wait and are watchful and are careful. We all worry, in small or big ways. We all try to cope, too. Maybe these letters are one of the ways I cope. Better that than a bottle or something worse. But we cope because faith can only take you so far.

The shadows follow us every day. Every remote alley and silenced car and wandering stranger is a threat. We don't take them lightly. We don't take anything for granted.

This is what I've been called to do. It's all I know, Mom. I sweat and bleed with these guys and that's all I can see doing. But in moments like this, in the stillness, I long for rest. Not physical sleep but emotional rest. I long to know what it's like to enjoy the peace we provide for others. I not only dream of experiencing the freedoms that Americans have. I dream of swimming in them and eating and drinking them up.

Fred Lewis dreamed of that too. He dreamed of that better place, that better life, that better day.

I think he's found it now.

But I don't want to know. Not like that.

I don't want to close my eyes and see Fred Lewis greet me.

I don't want to see Dad.

Not yet.

I want to serve and to believe that one day, I can let this go.

That I can participate in that dream.

I pray God will let me.

I pray for that one day.

James

————

An end always has a start.

It's now. It's time.

Beth knows she needs to let go of James, and the only way that can happen is for her to let go of all these letters.

She's not going to throw them away. She can't. But she's going to put them in the attic where they're not visible daily. Where she can't just slip a letter out and read it as if it's part of a newspaper.

It's finally time.

She wants to reread the only letter in here that isn't from her son. The one that started it all, this journey without a conclusion, this marathon without an end. The letter that came and told her the full story of what happened, the last letter to come since James was reported missing.

The handwriting is different, harder to read, but she has the words memorized nevertheless.

December 20, 2009

Dear Mrs. Thompson:

    I want to thank you once again. Not a day goes by without me thinking of what James did for me. Every time I wake up. Or look in the mirror. Or touch my daughter's hand. All these times it's hard not to think of James.

    Your son, Sergeant James Thompson, saved my life.

    I can still hear the sounds of the ambush along the steep trail in the mountains. I remember being hit, then remember the thought of them taking me away.

    All I thought about was the fact that I was going to die over there, in the hands of the enemy.

    Your son obviously had other ideas.

    It took more than courage for James to come after me into enemy fire. It took more than bravery. There's a strength there that is grounded by something else. I believe it's his faith and his upbringing. I got to know James a little out there and was impressed by his maturity. I know his family meant a lot to him. He was always carrying around one of your letters with him.

    After he brought me to safety behind a bluff and managed to call for help, he went back out. He engaged the enemy as I ended up passing out. And that was it. In a matter of minutes James and Francisco were gone.

    I know there is nothing I can say to give you assurance or hope. But I believe that James is alive and that we'll find him. We won't stop looking for the men who took him, the same men who tried to take me.

I know James was a praying man. Not all the guys out there are. I'd like to think that those prayers helped him. I sure know they helped me. I pray for James, in my own way.

Thank you for your gift in James. I will never forget what he did for me. I thank you. My family thanks you.

I hope for and look forward to the day I can personally thank James.

CPL Jesse Burks

PS: I've included a letter that James had written to you but not sent. It's dated August 21, 2009, shortly before he went missing. I hope the words are comforting to you.

———

It's time to say good-bye.

The mother thinks of his soft skin and hoarse cry and shaking hands. Holding him while he learned to nurse. His hunger and her determination. His wailing and her work.

The years blink and blow away.

She sits on the edge of the bed, a rumpled piece of paper in her hand, echoes of James's words rolling around in her head. Next to her rests a picture of him in uniform. Beth recalls James as a baby and what she used to tell herself over and over again while Richard was gone.

I won't be scared.

The first few nights, she *was* scared. She held James in her arms, wondering if she would have to do this alone . . . whether she would be a good mother . . . whether her son would love her and be proud of her . . . whether he would be everything she imagined he could be.

I won't be intimidated.

When he was a toddler, James used to hold her hand because he needed to make sure she was around. Nobody ever knew, not even his father, how tightly he held that hand of hers.

I will believe that tomorrow will come.

She recalls his different laughs and smiles. The bruises and cuts and the different cries that accompanied them. Then she thinks of his words in the letter.

I don't want you to worry.

The cool sigh of night blows through the spaces, the clean floors, the empty seats, the closed drawers, the cabinets of the house. The echoes rumble up the stairs and past vacant rooms to the four walls surrounding her.

I don't want you to wait for me in fear.

The paper feels light. As light as he felt in her hands the day he was born. As light as he looked riding his bike down their driveway. As light as his smile the day he left for Fort Benning.

I want to inspire hope in the guys around me. On the inside, where it counts.

Her hands shake.

It's okay, she tells herself. She closes her eyes. *It's all right to remember.*

Her fingers curl, tightening over the paper, crushing it. Both hands come together and scrunch the paper tightly. They remain tightened in two fists, compacting the thin paper.

No more letters.

The words remain here in this room in her heart and always will. She doesn't need to read them, just as she doesn't need to hold her baby to know. To remember.

The love.

The life.

He's not gone and will never be gone, just like Richard and Emily and Mom and Dad.

Beth falls back on the bed.

Her hand opens and the compressed page drops to the floor.

It's time even if I still don't know and maybe won't ever know.

She looks up at the ceiling. Vacant and open like the ocean. Colorless and shapeless.

It's okay.

She turns off the light and finds herself under the covers.

It's okay.

She closes her eyes and sleep comes.

It's okay.

And in the dream, he laughs as she sprinkles water over him in the baby bathtub. The water is warm and the giggle is low and the bathtub is blue and his smile is eternal.

It's okay, that smile says. *It's okay, Mommy.*

August 21, 2009

Dear Mom:

Some days I feel like I grow up a little more with each passing hour. I feel like the sun and the foreign soil and the threats all around weather and chap my heart and my soul.

Yet I write to you as someone softened and humbled.

I need reminders about the good things in life. I ask God for reminders. And today, I was reminded.

It was with the dry, hard palm of a little girl's hand.

I met her in the village I was patrolling with my unit. We were told that her whole family, parents and brother and sister, were killed in some bombings by the Taliban. She was just four years old and didn't have any idea what was happening. She looked at me with those chestnut eyes that seemed to ask me to take her home.

Maybe that was all in my mind, Mom. I don't know. The mind is a tool, shaped and trained just like our muscles. Sometimes I wonder how sharp and tough mine really is.

This little girl smiled at me even though she had nothing to smile about. Then she grabbed my hand and I swear it didn't feel right. It was so hard. So strong.

I don't know why she even grabbed my hand.

It made me think of our child that will soon be here. It made me think of Britt, of you, of all of you.

I think how easy it is for us back home to have our families and our comforts. This girl—this little precious soul—didn't have a family or a home to continue to make a life in. It had been obliterated. I don't know if she had been told. But I do know she managed to smile and laugh and even play like any other child might in the world.

It's easy to grow callous. To view all of these men and women and children as others, as "them," as something different from you or me.

This girl wasn't one of them.

Her name was Khatera.

The doubts I've had—the longings to go back home—the questions about the suffering and the violence and just the absolute hell of it all—Mom, Khatera reminded me of something.

I'm not in Afghanistan to carry on a Thompson tradition.

Or to be a hero here or back home.

She is why I'm here.

I think we're helping. And I continue to feel inspired to lead and to help and to fight.

One day, God willing, I'll be able to hold my son's or daughter's hand and feel their tender touch and know that I have the right to freedoms. To raise a family and to love and protect them. This is my hope.

So today, I pledge again to do my job and to inspire the

men around me. I want to be a light like this precious soul was for me.

Want to know what "Khatera" means? Someone told me it means "memory."

I'm never going to forget that sweet little smile or that name. And I pray I'm not going to forget why we fight.

Sometimes the world needs us to fight for them.

I look forward to talking with you soon. And seeing all of you again.

Love,
James

———

It is a Friday like any other.

Beth has been home for an hour after making the rounds at the Mountain Home VAMC this morning. She thinks of Murphy and misses him. It doesn't feel the same without his wisecracks. She's cleaning the kitchen after making a pie she will take to church tomorrow. The air smells of apples.

A day just like any other.

The windows are open and the autumn day is cool.

It's the sort of day when you need to be outside on the deck drinking a glass of iced tea, she thinks. A day for watching the kids play with the dog and talking to the neighbors.

A day to sit and relax and close your eyes and hold your spouse's hand for no other reason except it's there.

She hears the sound of a car door and wonders if it's Britt coming over to see her. But it's five o'clock. Britt is coming by later. She wipes her hands and then goes to the living room to look outside the window.

Then everything changes.

She sees the car and the figure getting out of it.

The uniform is all she needs to know that news is coming.

Sometimes all you need to see is a snapshot in order to know the rest of the story.

This is the day she's been waiting for the past two years. The day she's known would come, when the men would approach the house and knock on the door and deliver the news.

The news she's been waiting to hear.

The news she's been fearing.

God help me.

She doesn't realize it but she's already on the ground, the window no longer in view, the table blocking it, the chair next to her. She leans on it.

Tears like bullets are already unloading.

God, please.

Beth knows but she can't move. She can't get up, can't force herself to gain control, can't even think about saying or acting or doing anything.

All she thinks about is him.

She thinks of the blue blanket his grandmother made for him, the way he used to suck his thumb with the blanket wrapped around him.

She remembers his giggle and how he laughed uncontrollably when tickled. That sound—a toddler's laugh—might just be the first sound she hears after entering heaven's doors. That's how glorious it was.

She remembers his little voice and how he would ask her questions when he was just a few years old.

Those little mounds of cheeks. Those unwavering eyes like his father's.

A lifetime of memories flows through her.

The doorbell rings and she shivers.

Beth can feel her heart racing.

She tries to stand but feels light-headed.

All this time and I'm still not prepared? I'm still not ready? I'm still not willing to get up and find out?

She tries but she can't.

It doesn't matter if it's been two months or two years.

For nine months she waited and wondered and worried and then he was born. James Nathaniel Thompson.

For the next eighteen years, she watched and wondered and worried like any mother. She prayed and hoped and thanked God for every tiny miracle. Every step, smile, joy, and heartache.

Then he went into the army.

Beth has always known this: every soldier has a mom. And every mom can't help but worry and wonder. Mothers march with their children in battle. They are there in spirit. Even if they don't pray or believe in God, they're holding on to hope. Their hearts leave when their children are deployed. And they surely wait every day.

What's worse, the fighting or the waiting?

The doorbell rings again, prompting Beth to stand up.

He was a gift and it was his time and I'm finally going to know.

Then the door opens and she sees someone and shakes her head.

It's another dream. She must be in her bed taking a nap and dreaming. The man in the officer's uniform looks like her husband, except not really. He looks like both of them, the way James used to look, the way he appeared after coming back from Iraq, the boy who had blossomed into the man who would always and forever be her James.

"Mom?"

She feels her hands on her chest grabbing at a heart that might just explode.

Please don't let this be a dream, please, Lord, please.

"Mom, I'm home."

He comes to her side right before her legs give way again. He scoops her up and then embraces her.

"It's okay," he tells her.

"Tell me."

"Mom, it's okay. I'm here. I'm really here."

"Tell me."

"Tell you what?"

"Tell me you're really there."

"I am."

She looks up at James and sees his eyes and she knows. Dreams are never this vivid and this hopeful.

"I'm here, Mom. And I have several hundred letters to prove it." He smiles.

Something comes out of her but she doesn't know exactly what it is. It's not a distinguishable word or a sigh or a cry. It's something deeper.

Something comparable to gratitude.

You brought him home, Lord.

Beth goes to embrace her boy yet suddenly finds nothing there to hold on to.

She reaches out and her hands search in vain.

Suddenly the sound of the phone rings from all around her, and the picture starts to fade away.

No.

She opens her eyes and realizes the truth.

The undeniable, unrelenting truth.

No. The phone keeps ringing as she blinks and manages to sit up off the couch she's been sleeping on. It's Friday afternoon.

That's Marion on the phone.

She picks it up and clicks on the cordless without another thought.

"You're not going to believe the dream I just had," she tells her friend without even saying hello.

"Mom?"

It's Britt, speaking in a choked voice, on the phone. It wakes her up and makes her stand.

"What is it, sweetie?"

"Mom—they—I just heard—"

Her voice quivers and Beth opens her mouth slightly, knowing what her daughter-in-law is going to say, knowing that this is finally when the truth has arrived . . . and it is going to hurt.

"They found him. James. They found James. Mom—he's alive."

—

The engines roar to life and with the sound comes a sense of promise.

Yes, indeed, anything can happen.

"How are you doing?"

She could ask Britt the same thing.

"I could get used to this," she says from across the aisle. "Nice way for Richie to fly for the first time."

They're sitting in first class after a whirlwind twenty-four hours. On Beth's side next to the window is Emily.

The 747 they're on is headed to Frankfurt, Germany.

"So who would have thought *this* would be the way we got to Europe?" Emily says as she looks outside.

Beth clenches her hands and keeps hoping not to wake up. Yet she knows this is no dream, not like the one right before Britt called her to tell her they had found James and Francisco. They were alive, safe, and in stable condition.

Britt wasn't sure what "stable" officially meant, but

that's all the army had told her. They said they would be sending someone out to go over more details, which had happened yesterday at Britt's house while Richie and Bailey roamed around them making noises and acting like nothing was the matter. They had no idea that Richie's father had been rescued. They had no idea that he was now recovering at the Landstuhl Regional Medical Center near Landstuhl, Germany, along with Francisco DiGiulio.

Beth and Britt had embraced and the tears had seemed to never stop. Beth slept very little, first going to pick up Emily from college and then proceeding to tell family and friends. So many people—almost everybody, it seemed—told her how they had been praying.

Those prayers had been heard.

As the plane took off, Beth once again thought of the detailed plans of their trip. The army had managed to issue emergency passports for all of them, had given them a per diem to use while in Germany, had even covered all the bases like plans to pick them up from the airport and bring them to a place called Fisher House where they would stay.

"Mom?"

"What is it?"

"Why are you so quiet?"

"Just going over details."

"Isn't that why the army goes to the trouble of

doing it themselves? So type A personalities like yourself don't have to?"

"I'm not a type A."

"You are but you use that sweet southern charm to hide it."

Beth shakes her head. "You're such a smart aleck."

"And you love me."

She takes Emily's hand. "Yes. I do."

"I'm already nervous."

"I am too."

"All this time . . . I just hope he's okay. You know?"

She nods.

A part of her doesn't want to think about that.

There are so many things *to* think about. She's joyous and thankful and cautious and concerned and fearful and overwhelmed with humility.

Emily leans back in her chair and pops in earphones.

And for a while, a long while, Beth waits.

She knows there's something that she has to do.

It's time and she knows it.

———

Several hours into the flight, as Emily sleeps and Britt plays a movie for Richie on her laptop, Beth decides that it's time.

There was always hope when she read the letters

from her son. Always a tiny shred of hope that one day he would step back through her door.

Yet as Beth finally slips the letter out of her purse, she knows these will be the last words she will ever hear from Richard. On this earth and in this time.

Perhaps that is why she's never read the letter.

Now. Not tonight, not tomorrow, not next week.

We're not promised tomorrow.

She opens the letter and sees the familiar handwriting and feels as if Richard is right next to her, penning this letter as she stands over his shoulder.

My dearest Beth:

I'm not writing to say good-bye. I'm writing to make a promise.

I know that you're reading this after I've gone. We've talked about what that means—what will happen, what you will do, how you will go on—so I don't need to tell you everything again.

I'll just remind you of something.

I'll remind you that you are an amazing woman. And you're an amazing mother.

Sometimes I think fathers and men get in the way of raising children. Yes, God designed it so that the two can work as a team, but guys can be so clueless. It still surprises me that God created us first. Maybe he saw certain qualities that he missed so he designed something better, something more beautiful.

I know this, Beth. You are better and you are beautiful. And you will do fine on your own.

I don't think you're going to need encouragement for the next week, because we have so many loved ones who are going to surround you and the kids. I don't even think you'll need it for next month or next year.

I think you'll need it for down the road, for right around the time the kids are grown and about ready to leave.

I want to encourage you to live your life. To not only see the doors that open but to knock on them, too. I mean that about every aspect of your life, Beth.

I fear your being on your own and being lonely. That's the hardest thing about writing this and about leaving you.

Don't change who you are. You allowed me to be who I always wanted to be. Time on this earth—doesn't matter if we're allowed to live a hundred years—is as short as the crack of a gunshot. It's brief and powerful and then gone.

Continue to make yours count.

Thank you for allowing me to make mine count as well.

I served for you, for us, for the freedoms we have.

I was allowed to enjoy those freedoms, even for a short time. None of us know how much time we have.

So, Beth—I say this with a heart that's so full and so heavy. I want to hug you so hard and take you with me.

I don't know how it will work in heaven, what I will be able to do and say.

But, Beth, I promise you this: as much as I'm able to petition God the Father and His Son and His whole host of angels, I will do so on behalf of you and James and Emily.

And in whatever way I can—big and small, bold and subtle—I promise to protect and watch over all of you.

I believe I was called for a service and I don't believe that service has to end.

Whatever it takes in whatever way—that is my promise.

I don't need to remind you of this as I go—that I love you. But I do. I want to thank God in person for bringing such a remarkable, passionate, bright young girl into my life to be my rock and my heart and my anchor.

I will forever love you.

And I promise that I'll be waiting for you to make it home. And make it safe.

Richard

———

They enter the ward with the chaplain on one side and the military service liaison on the other. Britt is pale and won't let go of Richie's hand. Emily keeps looking at her and seems hesitant to move any faster than she does. They are quiet. So much has been said and talked about, but all they want to do is see James. They want to touch him and make sure he's real, he's okay.

I want to make sure he doesn't go anywhere ever again.

Beth doesn't think of the days that lie ahead. The celebrations and the parties and the ceremonies and the awards. The reunion with Marion and her family when they arrive later today to see Francisco. All she thinks about is this hallway and the room they're headed toward.

She can hear their footsteps on the floor.

Two years.

It's been two whole years.

"Richie, stay here," Britt says.

Yet Richie breaks free and starts running down the hallway.

They turn and then see the figure walking toward them.

For a second she doesn't recognize him. Not because James looks different, but because she's expecting him to be in a bed waiting and resting.

Instead, he's in his cargo pants and a long-sleeved army tee.

For a second, he stops, just as they do.

Britt gasps as Emily says his name.

James just stands there, tall and strong with a face that is more than surprised.

He's not looking at them, not just yet. He's staring at the boy who's racing toward him, a boy unknowingly racing toward his father.

James

I've died and gone to heaven.

The familiar phrase echoes in his mind and James really, truly believes that everything from that dusty day of hearing the gunshots to being lifted up in the air and soon tended to by men and women who spoke English was just a dream.

I passed away in some silent stretch of Afghanistan and this has been my journey toward the great beyond.

It's what he always imagined heaven would look like.

It's not the brilliant lights above and the glow of white surrounding him, though he is bathed in both.

It's the faces he sees coming down the hallway to greet him.

First he sees her, more beautiful than she looked on her wedding day, her eyes swollen with tears and emotion and love. Just waiting to be in his arms.

Next to them are the awestruck eyes of his little sister, who he's forgotten has turned into a young woman. The same little gaze that used to follow him everywhere and has managed to follow him here in eternity.

Then, of course, there are his mother's eyes.

Full of disbelief and hesitation. Yet also full of boldness and strength and resolve.

These three women walk toward him and he wants to bolt toward them with his arms open wide to embrace all three at once.

Yet he can't.

Because in front of them runs a face he recognizes.

In front of them bolts a little boy who must be somewhere around the right age.

A sweet angelic face that looks a lot like James's.

God, please let this be real.

The figure reaches him and for a moment James wonders if it's going to pass through him like a ghost, like those dreams he had on the field in the dead of night, when the angels would come and visit and tend to him, perhaps only in his imagination.

That touch and that giggle and that sweet precious little soulful voice are not in his imagination.

They are real.

James tries to say something but he doesn't even know the boy's name.

"Richie, this is your father."

The tears now feel heavier than they should, his vision covering for a while. He doesn't wait for the boy to come to him. He wraps his arms around the boy and starts to bring him up, then realizes something.

He is on his knees.

All this time and all these miles and all these prayers and all the strength it took to survive.

Yet here he is in front of the real warriors. And the angel accompanying them.

"Your father is home, Richie. Your father is here."

Heaven will have to wait a little longer. But hope is here to stay.

Beth

Britt left with Richie half an hour ago after the boy was sleeping in her arms. They won't be gone long, she tells them. Emily decides to go with them, leaving Beth alone with James. They've already been with him for three hours, listening to his story while sharing their own sagas of the past two years.

"I can't believe how big he is," James says. "I can't believe I actually have a son."

"He's been an amazing source of joy during all this."

It seems that "this" is something that James is still trying to wrap his brain around. He's told them some stories but been vague about others. The scars on his left cheek and neck reveal there's more to the story.

I wonder what scars remain deep down, hidden and unseen.

James sits on the edge of the bed, a television in the

corner playing news quietly. For a moment he looks at her as if trying to study her for the first time.

"What is it?" she asks.

"I never knew."

"You never knew what?"

"Do you know that when I got here, the first thing I did was start reading all those letters? They wouldn't let me call you but they gave me those letters."

"I sent a lot."

He shakes his head, then wipes tears from his eyes.

"I just knew," James says. "I kept telling myself that you guys hadn't forgotten about me, that you hadn't given up."

"We hadn't."

"There were times—oh man—but every time it seemed like a wave of peace would come. That if I was going to die, so be it. But I didn't dare just give in."

"I'm so sorry."

"All those things you said about you and Dad, about growing up, about losing him. The stuff about your faith in God. Man, Mom."

"What?"

James shakes his head. "How in the world am I ever going to be a parent like you?"

"You already are."

"No way. I just learned I have a son. It's still—this is all a bit surreal."

"You learn by doing it. What if someone asked how they were ever going to be a soldier like you? Someone who would give his life for another without a thought? That would be intimidating."

"It's different."

"No, it's really not, James. It's what's inside of you. It's your character. You just do what needs to be done."

"You know that I'm going to be an old man by the time I read all those dang letters?"

She sits on the bed beside him.

"I remember thinking after your father passed how much you changed. You weren't allowed to grow up slowly. God had other plans for you. I guess He had other plans for us all."

"One day I want to ask about those plans," James said.

"Me too."

She holds his hand and just lets the moment sink in.

After all the words she's written and shared, and all the moments she's sat and prayed, Beth now just sits in silence.

God brought her boy home safe and sound.

She wants to believe that Richard did what he said he was going to do in his letter. That he was watching out for James in whatever way he could.

One day I'll share that letter and that story with James. But not just yet.

"Thank you, Mom. Thanks for being here."

"Nothing was going to make me stay home."

"No. I mean—thanks for never going away. For never giving up on me. For staying close before, during, and after, no matter what happened."

Epilogue

THE FIRST LETTER

December 24, 2011

Dear Richie:

I've written ten thousand letters to you in my head and my heart.

This will be the first I'm writing by hand.

Your grandfather once said, "I don't write for today, I write for tomorrow." That's the beauty in letters like this, son. They're often for tomorrow. They're for pulling out and seeing and remembering.

I write these words for one of your tomorrows. And I'll start by saying it's been the greatest gift in the world getting to know you.

I prayed for a miracle when I was being held in the wilderness.

Little did I know that miracle would mean a smile as wide as yours.

This is my prayer now. That God grants us many more days and many more smiles.

When you become older, you might hear the words "hero" and "honor" when it comes to your father. But understand this—the true heroes are the ones supporting what we do. The true honor comes in faith in the system and in the soldiers.

I didn't come back a changed man until I realized how strong your mother and grandmother had been.

In my eyes, they are the heroes.

If anything, I aspire to be as strong as your grandma. And I hope to have the daily assurance your mother has.

I hope that you will know why I did the things I did, and why others are calling me heroic. But here's why I felt called in the first place.

I believe in this country and what it still stands for. There are those who want to tear it down on a daily basis. Yet there are those who stand strong and hold their heads high.

Be one of those, Richie. Don't let the cynicism of our times drag you down.

I hope you grow to be a strong man, yet I also don't want you to grow up too fast. I want you to be tough yet also keep a tender spot in your heart.

Know that no matter how dark the night may be, your father will always—always—love and protect you.

I will be here, watching over you.

Watching to make sure you're okay.

Love,
Your father

A Conversation with Mark Schultz

How did you come to write the song "Letters from War"? When did you first have the idea of using the song as the basis for a novel?

My great-grandma had three sons involved in World War II. My great-uncles have always been heroes to me. Several years ago as we were cleaning out her attic, we found the letters they had written her as well as her diary from the 1940s. Several of the entries brought me to tears, and I knew that I wanted to write a song that would honor both my great-grandmother and her sons.

What was your involvement in the U.S. Army's Be Safe— Make It Home campaign? Why was it important for you to be a part of the campaign?

The army approached me with the idea of making a video for "Letters from War" so that they could show it in conjunction with their Be Safe—Make It Home campaign for the soldiers in Iraq and Afghanistan. It was an amazing experience, and it has also allowed us to perform at the Pentagon as well as at several army bases around the country. Those concerts have been some of the most memorable of my career.

What can you tell us about collaborating with Travis Thrasher to write Letters from War? *What are some of the differences between writing a novel and writing a song?*

Well, I think we both learned a lot about the creative process and collaboration. Both Travis and I primarily do our craft without much collaboration, so it was interesting to meld our ideas together to make a compelling story. He was great to work with and did a good job blending our different styles. One huge difference between songwriting and book writing is the amount of work that goes into a book. A song may have 100 words as opposed to a book, which may have 30,000. But I think that writing this story has made me a better songwriter as well.

Early on in Letters from War, *Beth and her family gather to remember James on Memorial Day. Do you hope that the novel will inspire the public to honor our soldiers—and to keep them in their thoughts and prayers—more than one day of the year?*
Yes, I hope so. What I think this book does is connect you with the life of a military family in a way that lets readers experience it firsthand. I would hope that people look at these characters as real people because they are our neighbors, the ones who are dealing with these difficulties every day.

Your debut album, Mark Schultz, *was a hit with Christian music fans as well as with those of pop and country. Do you believe that* Letters from War *also holds a similar crossover appeal for different audiences of readers? How so?*
I have always said that what is real resonates. If a story is told well, it will make an impact in several genres. That is what I love about stories—they can transcend differences whether in music or in life.

There are so many poignant, powerful moments in Letters from War, *such as when Beth tells Britt that life doesn't always work out like it's portrayed in the movies. What is your favorite scene in the novel?*

Well, there are moments that are taken straight out of my great-grandmother's diary, and to me, those are the moments that make me the proudest. Also, the letter from the father to the son always makes me cry.

In the book you write: "Every soldier has a mom. And every mom can't help but worry and wonder. Mothers march with their children in battle. They are there in spirit." Why did you decide to have the song, and later the novel, feature the mother of a lost soldier rather than a father? Is Beth based on any one particular person? Do any of the other characters have specific real-life counterparts?

Yes. "Letters from War" the song and then the novel are based off my own family. My great-grandfather passed away from a heart attack before his sons went off to war, so that is why I focus on the letters from my great-grandmother to her sons. It was so moving to read the actual letters and see how much they looked up to and loved their father in those letters.

Beth draws on her belief in God for strength in dealing with James's disappearance. In what ways does Beth's faith reflect your own?

I certainly see Beth as a spiritually strong, and she is very real and honest with herself and with God. She struggles with this tragedy in her life that puts her faith to the test. I have never dealt with anything quite like that, but it is inspiring to me because I have had to learn in life to submit to God's will over my own. In Beth's case, she is learning to trust in God's will, whether that means she ever sees her son again or not.

As a successful musician you've had the opportunity to meet people from all walks of life. What were some of your memorable encounters with men and women serving in the military?

I performed one Sunday morning at the chapel of Lackland Air Force Base in San Antonio, Texas. They play the video of "Letters from War" every Sunday morning for the airmen. They all stand, put their arms around each other, rock from side to side, and sing the song at the top of their lungs. There is not a dry eye in the back of the room from the parents who are in attendance.

Later I performed the song for more than 5,000 airmen, and they sang so loud I just stopped singing and played the piano. Hearing the thundering echo of those voices throughout the church is something I will never forget.

What would you most like readers to take away from Letters from War?

I hope it brings awareness and a thankfulness for those men and women who serve in the military and the families that they leave behind. I also hope that Beth's faith will inspire readers.

Now that you have one novel under your belt, do you plan to write any more books?

My songs do lend themselves to being novels in that they are story songs. It has been fun to see how much more a song's story comes alive when you have more time to develop the characters and the plot. I love giving people a deeper experience of these songs.

FROM ONE OF CHRISTIAN MUSIC'S BEST STORYTELL

THE BEST OF

MARK SCHULTZ

a 17–song collection

Available now

WordLabelGroup
MarkSchultzMusic